Available in Norton Paperback Fiction

MANUEL PUIG

Tropical Night Falling

Translated by
SUZANNE JILL LEVINE

W. W. Norton & Company
New York London

Printed in the United States of America

Originally published in Spain by Seix Barral as *Cae la noche tropical*.
SIMON & SCHUSTER and colophon are registered trademarks of
Simon & Schuster Inc.

Quotations from Rubén Darío's "Sonatina" from Selected
Poems of Rubén Darío, *tr. Lysander Kemp (University of
Texas Press, Austin, 1965), pp. 52–53.*

Library of Congress Cataloging-in-Publication Data

Puig, Manuel.
    [Cae la noche tropical. English]
    Tropical night falling / Manuel Puig ; translated by Suzanne Jill
    Levine.
        p.   cm.
    I. Title.
    [PQ7798.26.U4C3413   1993]
    863—dc20   92-22612

ISBN 0-393-30908-8

W. W. Norton & Company, Inc., 500 Fifth Avenue, New York, N.Y. 10110
W. W. Norton & Company Ltd., 10 Coptic Street, London WC1A 1PU
    2 3 4 5 6 7 8 9 0

Tropical
Night
Falling

1

· There's such a sad feeling about this time of day, I wonder why?

· It's those late afternoon blues, when the sky starts getting dark, Nidia. It's best to keep yourself busy at this hour. Then, when night comes, it's different, the sensation passes.

· Especially if I can sleep well and not think about the terrible things that have happened.

· You're lucky that way, you don't know how it helps. When I can't fall asleep, that's when the most horrible things start going through my head. If it weren't for those blessed pills, I could never have made it through this whole period.

· You shouldn't complain, Luci. Your misfortune wasn't as great as mine.

· I know. But I haven't gotten away with anything either.

· When Mama died the same thing happened, remember? This time of day the memory of her would return, stronger than ever.

· Yes, as for that, we'd always remember her. But my first thought on waking up was that Mama was no longer there. That's when I missed her more than at any other time of the day. But back then, with so much to do, one didn't think as one does now, only about sad things. We had too many obligations.

· Always making meals.

· And the immense responsibility of the children, Nidia.
Of getting them off and running.

· And then to have something like this happen, to have
what you love most stolen away from you.

· Believers have some consolation. But as for me, I can't
deceive myself, I just can't. I really envy those who have faith;
it's a truly wonderful thing.

· Yes, Luci, I envy them too.

· Ignorant people have such an advantage, being able to
console themselves in that way. But we can't fool ourselves,
we see life as it is.

· When Pepe died it was different, I was in a state of
stupor. I cried and cried, all day long. This time it was different.

· A husband is one thing, Nidia, a daughter is another.
Your daughter. What a thing to happen, how awful.

· Luci, I don't want to be inside, let's go out for a walk.

· We can't now, it's about to rain.

· Luci, you didn't tell me about the woman next door.
Why hasn't she come back again?

· It must be because you came to stay here. She came
mainly to get things off her chest, but in front of you she
probably wouldn't dare.

· And she's young, she probably wants company her own
age.

· Why do you say that? No, she'd come all the time. You
can tell when somebody comes to see you because they really
want to. At first she didn't impress me all that much, but then
I got used to her. She's pleasant, in her own way, don't you
think?

· Look, Luci, I found her strange, but she's not a bad
person. She does keep her distance, though. Does she do that
with you too? Or is it just me?

· I think she found it hard because she didn't expect to
see you here and she'd come to tell me things. When she saw
you she couldn't.

· And that's why she never came again, Luci. You're the
one she wants to talk to, to try and get things off her chest.

· Look, Nidia, this woman had such high hopes. She was convinced that he loved her as much as she did him.

· But she's no spring chicken, she should know about these things already. Did she ever admit to you how old she was?

· No, but from her son's age and the fact that she studied before she got married, and got the degree that she did, she can't be less than forty-five.

· Almost Emilsen's age.

· How old would Emilsen have been in August?

· Forty-eight, Luci.

· How dreadful.

· It certainly is . . .

· But you have a son who adores you.

· Poor Baby. He's a good soul, but a daughter is a different story, Luci. That's something you have no idea about.

· You're crazy to be still calling him Baby, a fifty-year-old man.

· I can't help it. We always called him Baby.

· We'd better turn on the light now; dimly lit houses make me sad. I don't know if you've noticed, but old people's houses always have very little light. That's why I like to have everything well lit up. Didn't you ever notice that?

· Shall I turn on this one too?

· Yes, so it won't look as if somebody old lives here.

· And how did she meet the man?

· I already told you she'd been quite sick, right?

· Yes, Luci, but you didn't tell me with what. Was it the same as Emilsen?

· No . . .

· I thought it was, I don't know what put that notion in my head.

· No . . . It was something else, Nidia.

· You did tell me that she had a terrible scare.

· Yes, but they caught it in time.

· Then that's what it was, a tumor.

· No . . . What do they call it? It was a kind of virus. She explained the whole thing to me in Portuguese, using the terms the doctors use here.

· She often mixes up Portuguese and Argentine, I mean Spanish. I didn't get much of what she said.

· Well, she's been in Rio for years. When I'm talking to someone who's been here a long time, I also mix in a lot of Portuguese words without thinking.

· What was her illness, then?

· It was . . . some virus. They couldn't put their finger on it, the doctors, and when they finally figured it out the rest was smooth sailing. She met him there, in the hospital.

· What was wrong with him?

· His wife was in the hospital. She died, poor thing.

· Of what, Luci? Of the same thing as Emilsen?

· No, I think she'd had a stroke and was sick for a long time, but they knew she was going to die.

· How strange, a stroke in a young person.

· She didn't want to talk to me much about that. What she always wants to talk about is him.

· And he had a roving eye, at such a time?

· No, it seems he's a very good person; all he cares for is his home. He tried the impossible to save his wife, taking care of her all the time she was ill.

· So how did it happen?

· She saw him in passing there in the hospital, but always just in passing, in the corridors, when they'd take his wife out of the room for some treatment.

· And she was attracted to the man at a moment like that?

· No, you're getting ahead of yourself, because this girl isn't the kind who pays that kind of attention to men. What happened to her was very unusual, Nidia.

· Why?

· When she saw this man she thought she was seeing another . . . No, what I mean is that he looked a lot like another man in her life, whom she had loved deeply many years back and never saw again in her life. That was what really struck her. But she also thought she might never see the one in the hospital again either.

· The one in the hospital didn't look like her ex-husband, according to what you've told me.

· No.

· Then she's the kind that plays around, Luci.

· No, I don't think so. She works long hours and studies a lot. She's not always thinking about chasing some pair of pants, Nidia. Definitely not. You see, if you were right she wouldn't have been so bowled over by this one when he crossed her path.

· Well, I said that because there are already three of them in this story: the ex-husband, this one she met in the hospital, and the other one he looks like.

· From what I could tell, since her divorce she's been seriously interested only in the man from Mexico and now this one here, and that's all.

· Naturally, since they're an Argentinian, a Mexican, and a Brazilian it seems like more.

· Yes, the husband was Argentinian, had I already told you that?

· Was? Why, isn't he still alive?

· Yes, he's alive.

· You know, Luci, I can't get used to saying that Emilsen *was* this or that. That she's not here anymore.

· But she's here with you, present in your memory, and with all those who loved her.

· I don't buy that. Of course she's always going to be here present in my memory, but what do I gain by that? What I want is to talk to her, discuss whatever little thing comes into my mind with her, but I can't! I miss her, and she's not present at all.

· Nidia, it can't be any other way, it has to hurt, how can losing a daughter not hurt? Especially one who was always such a companion to you.

· I wish I could get used to the idea, gradually, that she isn't going to be there anymore. And follow the advice she gave me, because from the moment she fell ill, every time she had a relapse and saw how worried I looked, she'd stare into my eyes and say . . . "You'd better take care of your-self."

· The memory I have is when she was still healthy. With this distance from Rio to Buenos Aires, there was so much I couldn't experience firsthand.

· It's better that you didn't see her ill, though she never complained. But she looked so bad.

· What a girl, what courage.

· Luci, I'd be lying to you if I said that she let me see what she was going through. Never a complaint in front of me, nothing.

· What she wanted was for you to take care of your own health.

· I didn't want to come here now to Rio. I didn't have the strength, but I remembered what she'd told me, to take care of myself, and that's why I came.

· Look, Nidia, this has to be good for you. The beach, the cool air at night that lets you sleep well. The last time you came your blood pressure went down; the same thing will happen this time, you'll see.

· But the last time I was seventy-eight, and now I'm eighty-two.

· Ay, please don't mention those numbers, they sound like a joke, I can't take them seriously.

· They're no joke . . .

· Nidia, let's be more strict about our diet and your pressure will go down. If you lose a little weight you'll feel better.

· Don't make any more pasta, I can't resist those home-made noodles.

· The one next door loved them, though her background is Spanish and they cook more with rice.

· Why did she come to Rio?

· She left Argentina during the era of Isabelita and the Triple A, when they had that campaign accusing all psycho-analysts of being left-wing. She's not a psychoanalyst, but she's got a degree in psychology.

· I never understood that business, those diplomas didn't exist before.

· When I was a student the major didn't exist. Otherwise I would have done it. First you had to get a degree in medicine, and only then could you specialize in psychiatry.

· Yes, I remember that, Luci.

· And then they created psychology, for which you didn't have to study medicine, and that's where all those charlatans come from, may poor Silvia forgive me; after all, she's never been anything but nice to me. So now we have psychiatrists and psychologists.

· But you're leaving the psychoanalysts out in the cold.

· Well, according to Silvia herself, the title is psychologist, but when "psychiatrist" began to sound a bit old-fashioned, those who had studied medicine started to call themselves psychoanalysts. Something like that.

· Let's see if I've got this straight. Psychiatrists study medicine first, and psychologists don't study anything at all. And psychoanalysts are those who, because of one thing or another, want to give themselves that name.

· More or less.

· You see, I understood something, didn't I? Though you don't explain it well at all . . . My memory is starting to fail me, but if something is explained to me I can still understand.

· It's just that you have such good hearing. As for me, if more than two or three people speak at once, I don't understand a word they say.

· You shouldn't get mad at your son when he corrects you for that, Luci.

· Why?

· When you answer any which way, without being sure if you heard right or not, as if you were guessing.

· Look, Nidia, I think it's bad when one's children start acting like parents.

· Poor kid, he still worries about correcting you.

· Look, Nidia, I'm not going to be watching what I say to this one or that one, I say what I feel like saying and that's that.

· Well, all right, don't get angry. Tell me about the woman next door, why did she leave Argentina?

· I already told you, because there were threats from the three A's, remember? The Triple A Squad.

· Of course I remember . . .

· No, you just got through saying your memory's gone. See? You don't like people to be correcting you either. Well, she left because they called her one night telling her she had twenty-four hours to leave the country or else they'd kill her.

· Emilsen had a girlfriend who had to leave. But she was a university professor.

· Half of Argentina had to go. So she left her son with her ex-husband—they were already separated—and when the school year ended she sent for him. And he stayed in Mexico with her, the kid. He liked Mexico, and he's always told her that he wants to live there.

· I never went. We were going to go with poor Blanquita, but life didn't give her the time, poor soul.

· Nidia, have you noticed that all we talk about are the dead? How sad it is to be this age.

· Don't complain, Luci, please don't complain.

· You're right. Well, it was there that she met this man she fell so much in love with, and then she had to come back here because the altitude in Mexico was bad for her. And she's been here for some years.

· And the man who loved her so much didn't come with her? Why?

· She was the one doing all the loving. In the beginning he seemed to love her back, but not afterward.

· That's why the altitude started affecting her. You don't have to be a psychologist to figure that out. When I saw Emilsen was getting better, my blood pressure improved too. Sadness brings on all illnesses. But go on, I want to know more.

· Well, a few months ago she met this other man in the clinic, and he made an impression on her because he looked like the one from Mexico. But she never thought she'd run into him again, this one here. Until one day she goes to the Argentine Consulate to renew some papers and sees him. She goes up to him and greets him in Spanish and he laughs, because he's not Argentine. I'll explain. It so happens that before, in that clinic, there had been a very prominent Argentine medical professor who saw all his clientele there, folks like us, from the Argentine colony here in Rio. But he was already quite elderly and, as you can imagine, he's now dead. The point is that there in the consulate she saw this man and asked how his wife was, in Spanish, thinking that he was Argentine. Because they'd never spoken before. And he and the wife turned out to be Brazilian.

· So what was he doing in the consulate?

· Some transaction for a client. Pure chance. She says this man is very handsome, at least he is to her. She showed me a picture and I didn't like him at all, quite bald and a little pudgy. She says that was always her type of man, domestic, not too smooth-looking, and she says that she doesn't care if he has a little bit of a belly.

· And how was he like the other one?

· Don't get ahead of me. It took her a good while to realize it.

· But how were they alike?

· Their eyes. He had the same eyes. Dark eyes, on the small side, somewhat evasive; he wouldn't look straight at you.

· That's the look of someone who doesn't tell the truth.

· No, no. She says it's the look of a person who needs protection, like a little boy who's lost his mother. And that's what I told her: only children, particularly boys, have that in their eyes, when they're little, until they're twelve or thirteen, then they lose it and you no longer feel like hugging them close, squeezing them almost, for being so tender, the way they used to be.

· Girls are different, you're right. Or maybe it's just that Emilsen always seemed like a grown-up. The only thing about her that infuriated me was when she wouldn't sit still at the movies. She'd always have to go to the bathroom, anything to keep me from seeing the movie. But that was the only thing. She never gave me any other trouble at all.

· And my boys, who were a pain in the neck most of the time, would sit still at the movies.

· Go on. So she asked him how his wife was doing.

· Yes, Nidia. He told her that she had since died. They began to talk about the illness and about the other patients in the hospital; she too had been there about two weeks, and had been there awhile, in and out, some time before. She knew every case on the whole floor and the floor below because in earlier times that small clinic had been just a three-story house for one family. He began to tell her all this, and they talked awhile. She says he didn't look her in the eye much but kept looking at everything else, and she began to do the same out of nervousness. Though she hadn't realized it yet, he made her think of the other one, but she didn't connect the two and, like a silly fool, kept asking herself why, from the very beginning, this man had attracted her. In the hospital she'd often thought that there was something strange about the man in the corridor, something she liked but didn't quite understand. And there at the consulate, as they talked, he watched the people coming and going with their papers instead of looking at her, and when she too stopped looking at him, that's when she felt his eyes on her. He didn't get up the courage to let his eyes rest on her until she looked away. She began to feel his eyes moving all over her, her face, her hair, her mouth, her hands, her neckline. And when she decided to look him in the eye again, they would dart away. And there she got to observe certain details about him and noticed his shirt was wrinkled. It wasn't one of those shirts you wash and hang and they come out almost perfect, no, it was the kind that had to be ironed, and it wasn't ironed. That's when she suddenly couldn't hold herself back and the words poured out on their own: she suggested they have a coffee downstairs, in that shiny new mall where the consulate is. Because she's too restrained a woman. That's her problem according to her, she's too restrained.

· That's what I don't like about her, it just now hit me. She chews each little thing over too much, then she says just what has to be said and no more.

· Yes, there's nothing spontaneous about her. I told my son, and he tells me that Argentine women today are like that, too dry. That's because the mothers were so talkative, and not very sincere, you know, trying to act charming with everybody.

· We were false, you mean.

· Not false, but professionally charming, Ñato says. And this woman is the new wave.

· No, the young girls are the new wave. This one is older.

· I mean she's the new breed. But that day the man shook her up; something he communicated to her made her speak before thinking, like the thing about going to have a drink. Anyway, he answered that he had very little money on him, and she said she'd treat—a soft drink or something for her, because coffee jangles her nerves, she never drinks it unless she has patients back to back and has trouble keeping her eyes open. Well, the man accepted.

· Luci, you sound like you were born yesterday.

· Why? Do you think she's not telling the truth?

· It looks that way to me. She's the kind that plays around. She probably doesn't want you to know more about her than this affair, but I'll bet she has one like it every so often.

· Why are you always so evil-minded?

· I'm convinced that that's the way it is.

· No, Nidia, she's very frank about these things. She's always telling me her biggest defect is that she's rather old-fashioned and can't have anything with a man unless her heart's in it.

· Go on.

· But if you're not going to believe anything she says, why do you want to know more?

· Is she completely cured now?

· She says so.

· She looks good, so at least that much must be true.

· According to her, she was sure she wouldn't make it. She felt so bad off that she was certain there was no cure. So when the doctor told her she was out of danger, a kind of madness, a euphoria, came over her, a stronger desire to live than she had ever felt before. And when she got back to her apartment she started to think about that man in the hospital and wonder why he had made such an impression on her. She says that in those moments she wished she were able to draw well enough to sketch his face from memory, to study it and understand why he had impressed her so.

· Tell me how he looked in the photo.

· He's no movie star. He's bald, stocky let's say, very wide shoulders. A little fat, not flabby, though. A bit of a belly. But from her own description I had imagined him differently: taller, strong but not fat. According to her, everything is in his eyes and his voice.

· Luci, you were right, it's starting to rain.

· The eyes of a very sensitive person who is easily affected by things, or can be affected, even hurt. And the voice, because it's very deep, she says, with a beautiful resonance, like you might hear in a church. And that's not all: deep down she noticed a kind of tremor.

· So then she had already talked to him in the hospital. She didn't lose her touch even when she was ill.

· No. That's the thing she keeps repeating. She already liked him from afar, and not for any obvious reason, because he's not a man that people normally would look at twice. Even once she'd left the hospital she kept thinking about him, as if he were lost to her forever. But I'm explaining this badly. What she kept wondering was: why had she liked that man and why couldn't she put him out of her mind? She still hadn't realized that he looked like the other one. But as soon as she found him again by chance in the consulate there, she began to perceive something. It was as if she'd been given a pencil and was drawing a man—the other one from Mexico, the one she loved so much—drawing him as the most skillful illustrator would, and he was coming out with the exact resemblance, that same tender child look in his eyes, but without the defects of the one in her past, who was an ordinary-looking, skinny blond fellow. This one, no, he was not someone to crumble easily, no matter how hard the worst of all winds blew, the winds of misfortune, and sadness.

$$2$$

· It was her, right?

· Yes, she says hello. She asked how you were.

· If she only knew how I criticize her . . . Poor thing, sometimes I talk just to hear my own voice.

· She's never let so much time go by without giving me a call. I think she wanted to come by to tell me something. Or, more likely, to tell me the same old thing again, because she hasn't heard from him.

· She probably called to see if you were alone, to see if I'd gone out.

· That's possible. Obviously, she's quite obsessed with this matter.

· But, Luci, doesn't she see patients at this hour?

· Yes, but one woman called to say she couldn't come. And she had forty-five minutes free, so she decided to lie down for a bit. See, from this window you can see her window. Come look, it's that one up there on the third floor, the bedroom window. The office faces the other side. I always know when the shutter is down; I know if she raises it early on Sunday or sleeps on till twelve. Now the shutter is always raised from early in the morning, she can't just lie around all morning when she's not working. It's because of her nerves.

· But her health is still good? Did she say anything about that?

· No, she's fine. It's just that her head is spinning too fast. I think she's a good person, which is why so many patients go to her. She knows how to help people, she genuinely cares about them. And she thought she could help that man. All because of that one special moment down there in the new bar at the consulate. Here in Rio sit-down bars aren't in fashion; people have drinks on the run, standing at the counter. That's why there's almost never anybody in the new bar down in that elegant building. It's nice and quiet and there's a cool breeze, none of the rushing around you see in that hellhole of a consulate. Anyway, he couldn't look away, and neither could she, because they were sitting opposite each other at a nice little table.

· Is it outside or inside, like a café in Buenos Aires?

· In Buenos Aires there are also cafés with tables on the sidewalks. That's what I miss from there—at every other step there'd be a bar where you could sit awhile.

· Luci, I'm glad you realize there are good things about Buenos Aires. Anyone listening to you would think Rio de Janeiro was the only place in the whole wide world.

· Don't exaggerate, Nidia. It's just that Buenos Aires brings back bad memories. To think I had my wonderful house there, and lost it. That didn't happen to you, losing your house and everything, down to the last cent.

· A lot of people have lost everything in these years.

· But when foreigners go to Buenos Aires they love it. Especially all the cafés you can sit at. You can spend hours with a cup of coffee and no waiter comes to pressure you to leave the table or to order something else. It's a custom we have only there, spending hours sitting and talking.

· You remember in Italy how much it cost to sit at a café, it was a luxury.

· We inherited that custom of ours from Spain. They spend their lives talking. I don't know how that country has progressed so much; all they do is chat away.

· One day will you take me to a café? I don't know any in Rio.

· I'll take you, but it's not the same. They're more beer places, which is why only young people go, if not just men. Ladies don't go, it's too wild. Rio isn't for senior citizens; as you saw for yourself on the beach, we were the only ones.

· So where do the old people hide?

· What do I know? . . . They lock themselves up at home, Nidia. People must think I'm crazy, out on the street all day long.

· If only you *were* out on the street all day long, Luci. That way you'd take me out for a little fresh air. Sadness comes over me here indoors, it seems.

· Nidia, when the weather's good there's not a morning I don't take you to the beach, but twice a day tires me out. You're indefatigable.

· That girl looked bad to me this morning. Not at first, but this morning on the sidewalk she didn't look good. I hope she's not having a relapse.

· I think it's because she isn't sleeping well. Her mistake was to have gotten her hopes up so high.

· But why did she get so stuck on him? What did he promise her?

· Nidia, it's just that they were starting to get along so well things looked like they were going full speed ahead. In the bar there he told her about his work, his children.

· Luci, do you think my son-in-law is going to marry again soon?

· Look, Nidia, the more you've loved somebody the more you suffer their loss and the more you need to replace them. He adored Emilsen, and frankly I hope that he finds a good woman soon to help him. He's not even fifty yet. Remember how hard it was to be alone at that age.

· By that age I was already used to being a widow.

· But men are different, they can't be without a woman.

· Luci, that man, had he been happy with his wife? What did he tell this other one?

· That he was desperate. That the first days he'd felt a great relief because the poor dear wasn't suffering any longer but that now he was going out of his mind.

· And who takes care of his kids?

· She'd been sick so long by then that he'd already solved any problems with the kids. He found an older lady to do everything for him. And besides, the kids are already grown, seventeen or something like that, the girl's the youngest. And they all live together with his mother. But our woman next door realized immediately that he was a very good man, because she had seen him in the hospital bringing his paper work with him to get ahead while he kept his wife company. Naturally she was left wondering, what kind of papers? In the bar he'd told her that he was a bookkeeper, or accountant, she told me in Portuguese, specializing in taxes. And he'd take all that work with him to the hospital after a long day of hustling and bustling downtown.

· How do you know?

· This poor Silvia found it all out afterward. He's not well off, and he has to work as much as he can. Imagine, with the mother and two youngsters at school. He was able to take his wife to that clinic because she had health insurance from her job as a high school teacher. Well, they were in the bar and right there the man asked this Silvia if that was why she wanted to talk to him, if she wanted him to do some work for her. She was taken aback, because the man came out first thing with this. He thought she'd known since the hospital that he was an accountant. Only then did she ask him what kind of work he did, and he told her. And she said no, that she only wanted to talk to him, to know about his life. There it seems he couldn't meet her eyes, and he looked the other way. And he began to tell her that his was the most humdrum life in the world; what could he possibly tell her so as not to bore her? And there she was even more taken aback, so she told him that she felt she was beginning life again; she had thought she'd never be cured, and had decided to be more communicative than ever before. She wanted to talk to him because it seemed that he too might have the need to communicate something. Those things one says that aren't the truth.

· What was the truth, Luci?

· Well, you'll remember, when one has that youth inside, that health, it makes you feel like getting close to someone you like. That's all, she liked the man, period, who knows the reason, but she felt that desire to know about him, who he was, what he liked. She told him no more than that, that when she knew she wasn't going to die she had made the promise to be more open, not to close herself off foolishly, to live another way. But of course what she didn't say was that instead of addressing just anybody—for instance, that skinny, unfriendly receptionist at the consulate—she had approached him. Because something about him attracted her. Of all the thousands of men who passed by as she got better, she chose him. She says he answered all her questions, was attentive but held back a little. Like someone who hasn't quite woken up, still half asleep in the early morning. He spoke, but something deep down inside him was still asleep, she felt. She asked again what his life was like. It was a very sad life, because it seems that his wife's insurance didn't cover all the expenses of her illness. He made the wife believe that the insurance paid entirely for that clinic, for a private room and the best of care, but that wasn't true. He fell into debt, and now he's having to pay. The trouble is, there's not enough time in the day to do all he wants to do. The more clients he has the better, but a day has just so many hours and no more. And there in the consulate he was doing God knows what transactions, all of them very trying, researching some tax agreement between two countries for some rich client who doesn't want to pay his taxes. The point is that his life is no more than that, working from morning to night and coming home and finding everything in order, thank God, because his mother still has the strength to watch over things a little.

· But does the mother have other help, a sleep-in, or not?

· No, they have that older lady who comes every day until the afternoon, but she leaves once the kids' dinner is ready. The mother washes the dishes at night. So he finds everything in order. This Silvia imagined how sad coming home might be for him, so she went and brought up the subject. And he let it all out. The mother watches television all day, so by ten P.M. she can't keep her eyes open anymore. He asks her to wake up later in the morning so that she won't be so sleepy at night and they can talk a little. But you know how at this age one can't sleep after a certain hour. And if the old lady has coffee at night she won't be able to fall asleep, so what's the poor thing going to do?

· She's not even her mother-in-law yet and this one next door is already saying bad things about her. Is she telling you the truth? I don't believe her.

· What would she gain by lying to me? He never gets home before nine, and then he takes a shower to clear away some of his fatigue, especially in his head, and that's when he'd like to chat a bit with his mother about what happened during the day with the children. But you can't get the old lady away from her eight o'clock soap, and as soon as that garbage is over, her son asks her to watch the news so she can bring him up to date on what's going on. But the old lady's already tired when she's watching the news and doesn't remember a thing, worn-down old woman, one shouldn't let oneself go like that! Let yourself go and you've had it. Nidia, don't you ever stop reading the newspaper and watching the news.

· That's right, in Argentina I always watch it on TV; when Pepe was alive we'd do it all the time, listening to the news on radio.

· The man puts on his pajamas and all day he hasn't had time to reflect on anything, running around downtown Rio from one office to another, but there at the end of the day he has no one to talk to. The main thing for him is to find out what the kids have been up to; his wife would always give him all the details. One day he got very serious with the old lady and said to her that if she didn't waste her eyesight watching TV she'd be more awake when he came home, and that he was going to sell the TV set. The old lady broke down crying. And right then and there he almost died of regret, because he realized his poor mother was all worn down and didn't have any more energy for confrontations; he was the one who had to stand strong. So while he eats, the old lady tells him a few things, but she's already falling off her feet she's so tired, and that's his life, according to this Silvia . . .

· Why do you always say "this Silvia"?

· Because there's the other one, in Copacabana, the journalist, who you still don't know and who is also Argentine.

Anyway, luckily he starts feeling tired—before dinner no, but after he fills his stomach the fatigue hits him. There are days he falls asleep before the old lady. But not on those days, especially Saturdays, when he doesn't get up so early. On Saturdays before his wife fell ill, if sleep didn't come over him they'd try watching some movie on TV. They couldn't stand so many commercials, though, and his wife would take advantage of the commercials to make comments to him. But now, nothing. They'd argue because his wife would insist that it's better to have the light on while watching TV, that it's better for the eyesight, according to some article she'd read somewhere. But he preferred to be in the dark, like at the movies. He told all these details to this Silvia, because even though he had gotten along well with his wife, they weren't completely happy.

· When was it that he began criticizing the wife? In the bar at the consulate?

· Don't make me lose the thread. Because now he can get away with putting out all the lights, and yet when the commercial comes on he has to remember she used to be there, and with the light on, because she was very insistent about that. And he was always asking her to be a little better dressed at night when he came home, and when the commercial would come on and she'd look so shabby he'd tell her she looked like a beggar, and maybe she did it on purpose so that on the days when she did fix herself up a bit he'd notice and pay more attention to her during the commercials, because once, for her birthday, he'd bought her a dress that was a little more expensive and she was saving it for a special occasion to impress him. But the dress he liked most, for the way it looked on her, was one he ordered from a friend who'd gone to New York, but for his mother, because she was turning seventy, and when it arrived the dress was too small and so of course the wife inherited it. Apparently this dress transformed her, it looked so good on her, with a green and white flowery print. And she would wear it so little.

· And this Silvia saw the dress?

· No, he never took her to his home. She says she's going to be very careful never to put on anything green and white for him. On the back of the dress it said clearly "dry clean only," and to save money the wife tried to wash it at home, with the most delicate soap, but she ruined it. He never forgave her; whenever this subject came up they always fought because, trying to save on dry cleaning, she'd also ruined a pair of his pants, Italian linen pants that weren't really linen, which is why they required special care to clean, they must have been a mixture of linen and synthetic fibers.

· But now she's not here anymore, not in her green and white flowers nor in anything. I think that if he told her all about the wife it's because he wasn't interested in this other one as a woman.

· It seems strange to me too. He seems to me to need a friend, a confidant, more than a lover. But I didn't dare tell her this.

· You did wrong, it's better to set her straight once and for all.

· No, Nidia, you wouldn't dare tell her either. You'd feel sorry for her. Besides, when she's telling you everything it seems that she's right, that he does love her. And she tells you the whole story with all sorts of details until you're convinced.

· Did you ever catch her in a lie? She doesn't contradict herself?

· No, she's told me everything from beginning to end God knows how many times. It's the only thing that gives her relief.

· She must be afraid she'll never see him again.

· And for him it's better to have the lights off, there in the living room—don't you agree?—when the commercials come on, so he won't see the empty seat, better that he see the commercials. And at that hour he's always fresh out of the shower, smelling of those nice perfumed soaps they have here in Brazil. This Silvia didn't tell me that, nor could she know it, but I can imagine the pajamas weren't ironed, like that shirt the other day. Still, there in the dark that man alone, bald, with a bit of a belly but all smelling of soap perfume, must have some hope for something in life, on a Saturday night.

· And besides, he must have that problem, that electric charge in his body . . .

· . . . in a man who's still young, Nidia.

· And the children aren't there?

· They're not even there on weekdays, let alone Saturdays. But they don't give him any trouble. It seems that before the wife fell ill there were a lot of goings-on in the house, because the daughter was always coming home late at night, one of those wild little Brazilian girls, typical of today. The boy was more easygoing, involved in sports. Though he's very sorry, the father I mean, that he can't buy him the surfboard he promised him. Do you want to know something? The woman next door was about to buy him the board when the man disappeared. How I hate those surfers. Besides, they live far from the beach, not like us who are almost facing it; why did that kid want a board so much?

· I hate them too. The nerve they have; all of a sudden they'll be all over you like a bolt of lightning, such nerve. I'm there in the water, just a few feet from the shore, and they come crashing in and look at you as if you're in their way. I don't even see them until they're nearly on top of me!

· On the other hand, that way they blow off a lot of steam, those young boys, better that way than with drugs. So the thing is, he doesn't see his kids too often.

· And before the wife got sick what happened? You started to say something.

· Yes, a lot was going on at home, the girl being so young and already living the life of a woman, you know what I mean. And the boy wasn't a good student, but when the mother got sick the family became closer. And that continued after her death. The grandmother got used to her granddaughter's dating, and since the girl doesn't neglect her schoolwork everything is calmer now. It seems she has a steady boyfriend now, a classmate. The point is that this man comes home at night dead-tired, to his mother watching television, and she reheats the food the servant has cooked.

· And this Silvia asked him what his life was like? How'd she get up the nerve? Or did he just tell her?

· What's so bad about asking?

· A woman shouldn't ask such questions. She's a psychologist, so she should know that. It's what worries me most about my son-in-law—and, Luci, you know very well what men are like, the problems they have. Men aren't like us, especially at that age, still young.

· But, Nidia, if you're going to measure everything you say, best to just wear a gag.

· My fear is that Ignacio will get married again to the first woman he comes across, out of that need a man has for a woman. Men are like that, Luci, it's their nature. I know it because when I'd get sick sometimes, Pepe would have that problem. He couldn't sleep if he spent a few days without it.

· But your son-in-law really loved Emilsen; that suffering must, I think, kill everything, the desire to go out, to have fun, all that.

· You're wrong, Luci. Didn't you just say this other man couldn't sleep Saturday nights? It's for them what hunger is to us. I myself, the very day Emilsen died . . . I barely had the strength to stand up. And then Ignacio insisted I eat something; I have to admit it did me good to eat a little. I was hungry that day, leaving the wake to go home for something warmer to wear since there was almost no heat in the funeral parlor, those thieves. That's how it is, my life was over when Emilsen left me, but even so, hard as it is to believe, I felt cold and hungry. And when I put something on I had more strength to confront things. Because on an empty stomach, and not dressed right, I'd begun to get anxious and feel like screaming and jumping out the window, but Emilsen's kids, poor things, were there and it wasn't right to make a scene in front of them, so with the coffee and bread and butter, and the nice cardigan we bought together in Rome, I got my strength back.

· You're right, Nidia. What this Silvia must have wanted to know deep down was how he had resolved that problem. Which has nothing to do with his ongoing love for his wife. Or maybe I'm wrong. You know, I just thought of something. If he loved the wife a lot, he might end up completely paralyzed, without a drop of energy left at night when he goes to sleep in his bed alone. Or maybe he didn't love her all that much and got over her death almost immediately. But it could also be that he loved her terribly and can't think of anything but her, and he's so desperate that to keep from bursting from all the pain growing inside him and already bigger than him, well, he could do something crazy, like jump from the tenth floor, or go off with the first tramp who crosses his path.

· You're thinking the same thing I am. I'm afraid Ignacio will do just that.

· Well, the first day they talked a lot, about his kids, nothing about the wife yet, nor about the dress, none of it. And at one point he stared at her and smiled, and said that he'd been different as a young man. That in the past he'd had another kind of life, when things were different in Rio and money wasn't so scarce. In those days he'd been something of a loafer, even a bit of a rebel. But that was all ancient history now, and he felt ashamed not to have anything but tales from the past to tell her. Because the present was for him like a . . . I don't remember the word Silvia used.

· It must have been a calvary, that's the word I would use.

· No, it was something else . . . the barren moors! Though for me, Nidia, when I say moor I think of the Brontë sisters. For me the moors may be gray but they're an interesting place, with a sense of mystery, a white mist, and at times something more, you remember? Gusts of wind and rain with the sun shining through, how that happens I don't know. And those threatening low dark clouds. Remember our excursion to the Brontë Museum? Instead of moors, he should have said vacant lot.

· I don't remember that museum, Luci. What's been most affected is that, my memory. What excursion was that?

· Let me continue with this other thing, then I'll tell you about that trip, to the moors of *Wuthering Heights*.

· Oh yes, I remember *Wuthering Heights*, where you could see something weird, far away, as we came out of the museum.

· Right, a mirage; it looked like a house, lost out there where the moors begin.

· It's not true, there's nothing there. It's land nobody wants.

· See how you remember? I always go back and review the brochures of every trip we take, you have to exercise the memory. But she told him that she knew the things going on inside him were not run-of-the-mill. She wanted to know how he saw the future, if he still had some thread of hope.

· She kept going around in circles, Luci, but what she wanted to know was one thing: if he had that animal drive, that need to be with a woman.

· I don't think so, Nidia. That's part of the reality, I don't deny it, but first and foremost what this Silvia wanted to know was if he still had any illusions left in life. Secretly hoping, of course, that she could share those illusions with him. And there she got up the nerve—maybe because she has so much experience with her patients—but the point is, she suddenly stood firm and asked him why he always looked away, what was the reason to be ashamed? And he answered that he didn't understand why she would be interested in what happened to him, with the dull life he had. If she was investigating cases like his—a man of forty-odd years, a widower with grown children—she should go ahead and ask whatever she liked. But since, as you know, she didn't have the slightest intention of investigating anything as a professional, she made that fact quite clear to him. That's when he seemed to come out of his stupor. How could anyone possibly take note of him?

· Excuse me for interrupting you, but what did we do when we came out of that museum of those girls who were writers?

· Emily and Charlotte Brontë, don't you remember their names?

· No, but remember, I've always been bad with names. You used to laugh because I'd . . . who was that actress whose name I'd get wrong and you'd always laugh?

· Barbara Stanwyck, you called her Barbara Stavisky. After that famous crook named Stavisky.

· What a memory you have for names! No, it's not names I mind forgetting. But now I'm also forgetting things that happened. And I don't want to forget anything, especially the good things. The good moments, ever since Emilsen was born up to the day she felt the first symptom. How was it? Did we or didn't we walk into that field with thorns everywhere, after we left the museum?

· No, we could see the mirage, but it was too far to walk to reach what only looked like a house in ruins. I think the house really does exist. They call it a mirage on purpose, so that people don't go there and get lost in those endless moors.

· I thought so too, that there was something there. But yes, it's land that isn't worth anything, that never gets sold, where nothing grows. Why would anyone build a house there among the thorns, so far into the badlands? Better to build it on the edge of good land.

· They say that Emily Brontë would sit for hours and hours and gaze out at the moors, wondering why a man had built the house so far away among the thorns, and imagining what he would be like. She thought it must have been a man who had suffered a great deal, who had had nothing but disillusionment from people, that's why he wanted to isolate himself like that. She must have wanted to get close to him, but probably by then all that was left of the house was in ruins. To get close in order to help him.

· And this Silvia who wanted to help the man found herself sinking into a mire. But she didn't want to help him, Luci, she wanted to complicate his life. She wanted to have a little fun, and she didn't care if in the process she intruded into the life of someone with open wounds, so difficult to heal. She was a daring, irresponsible hussy. She'll just have to live with it if it all backfires on her.

3

- Luci, I'm having a bad day.
- It's the weather. If it weren't raining we could go out a little.
- Would it be hard to get a taxi?
- Yes, impossible more likely. And the streets might be flooded, it would be crazy to go out on a day like today.
- It's just that being cooped up like this makes my memories come back.
- Make me a maté, Nidia. Put very little sugar in yours.
- I'll just take it bitter. But don't tell me what you always do, you always say the same thing when that subject comes up.
- What is it I say to you?
- That life already gives us enough bitterness. But you, Luci, should accept things a little more.
- I can't, Nidia.
- You have two healthy sons. One lives a block away, and the other is way down in Buenos Aires, but you know he's well.
- I want so much to see him.
- He's not coming this summer?
- He's low on cash, you know how things are now in stinking old Argentina.

· Poor Argentina. You don't feel like going there?

· Poor thing, he works all day, his wife works even more. What am I going to do, the whole day alone in that house?

· They still have all those cats?

· Even if they spent more time at home I wouldn't set foot there; you know how terrified I am of cats.

· How many do they have?

· I don't know, around ten. They're crazy. It's almost as if they kept them on purpose to stop me from going.

· He misses you a lot; he's a very affectionate kid. When I'm feeling my worst I call him up and we talk a little. He misses you a lot, he misses your cooking, the affection.

· He has that terrible arthritis, barely forty years old and arthritis already.

· Luci, please! God will punish you, whether He exists or not. You exaggerate too much! If little Luis works all day and plays tennis twice a week, he can't be that bad off. Don't exaggerate all the time, and always for the worst.

· Don't fill the kettle all the way, or the water will never boil.

· You're right. I was distracted, thinking about something else.

· About what?

· About what I was telling you, that God will punish you.

· God punishes with neither stick nor whip, remember that saying?

· The neighbor didn't call?

· No. A sign that there's no news. I think she's embarrassed to talk about him now. The last time, she repeated the whole story about that happy weekend they spent together.

· With all the details?

· Juicy ones, you'll be scandalized.

· No, I won't. I say let people do what they want, live their lives while they can. Other things seem more important to me than they did before. Life teaches you to give importance where it's due.

· She told me everything without leaving out a single detail. I even know where they went.

· I don't care one way or the other about that. What I am

curious to know is at what moment he accepted the idea. Of going out with somebody. It makes more sense for a man to go to a bordello if he has a sudden attack of that fever—to deal with a woman he doesn't know and will never see again. That poor creature could never take the place of his wife. But with this Silvia, I don't know, he couldn't have thought of her in the same way he'd think of a woman in a bordello, a means of relieving himself. When did they see each other again, after the café?

· She says that when she got up from that table in the bar she already knew that she really liked him.

· Luci, but women in a bordello don't . . .

· Nidia! What bordello? They don't exist anymore! The women are all over the place out there, that's all. The streets of Rio are filled with that kind!

· Don't shout at me like that, I'm not deaf like you! What I mean is that those on the street, they cost money. Maybe he preferred this Silvia because it wouldn't cost him anything.

· No, it wouldn't cost him a thing. She was the one who picked up the tab, you'll see.

· But before that, tell me when exactly he brought up the subject of the flowery dress. Because that was where he began to criticize the poor woman who had just died.

· No, he didn't say it as criticism. You're putting words in my mouth, and what's more you're confusing me. I want to tell it as she told me, this Silvia, without forgetting anything.

· I want to know one thing and that's all: when did he break down? I mean when was it that he said to himself, I'm going to take up with this woman chance has brought me?

· I don't think he realized. Before he knew it he was involved. She told me so later a thousand times, when the crisis came, when she was trying to analyze his withdrawal. A strange withdrawal that came afterward. Let's take it step by step. Everything began in the bar downstairs in the consulate. Saying goodbye, he was already acting strangely, as if he had been deeply impressed; I already mentioned that.

· What do you mean by impressed?

· She explained it to me clearly, but right now I don't know how to describe it to you. When I see her I'm going to bring it up. There's nothing she likes better than to talk about this. Anyway, right then she had an idea: there was going to be an art opening downtown within a few days, at the beginning of the following week, and she had been invited to a cocktail party. As his work kept him downtown, she thought that he'd likely be there at seven in the evening and they could go together. This was on a Thursday or Friday, and the cocktail party was on the following Monday or Tuesday. He said yes, that he wanted to go, so that they could continue talking.

· And he didn't have to pay for her drink, because it was free.

· They left it that he would call her to confirm that very next Monday morning, or Tuesday. But according to him, it was almost certain that he'd be able to go. They said goodbye with a warm handshake, and he gave her a big smile, with his lips spread, which made her think that he was quite pleased. Quite pleased to have met her again.

· Only he smiled, not her?

· I don't know. Knowing her as I do, I don't think so. She was probably concentrating on giving him all the information: the place of the art show, the time, the fact that it was right around the corner for him, very convenient, easy to get to, very close by, just around the corner from those horrible offices downtown where he went to do his accounting.

· She smiles very little. It's so serious, her expression.

· She's serious inside too. It seems that returning home from the consulate, without realizing it she began to walk and walk instead of taking a taxi. She felt so light, as if she had wings and only needed to unfold them for the wind to carry her, for her to glide among the clouds, the wind at her back. Though "the wind at her back" brings a bad memory to mind.

· Which one?

· No, I'll tell you later. Let me continue with this. She couldn't understand why she felt so good, why life looked wonderful. What kind of power did that man have? Why had he had such a strong effect? He hadn't said anything particularly sensitive, or intelligent, nothing, but he had left her with a terrific desire to see him again. Why?

· She had probably already realized that he looked like the other one.

· Not completely, wait. And that same night . . . a theatrical touch! It's ten o'clock or later and her telephone rings, she answers, and it's him! He gives her the excuse that he's not sure he took down her number correctly. And they talked around two hours. They couldn't hang up. In his house the mother had already gone to sleep. That's when he told her about the flowery dress, about everything I already told you. But he still wasn't sure he could make the date. He was going to call her on such and such day, at such and such time.

· He did wrong to confide so much.

· That weekend she had a good time; she changed some furniture around and did things she had wanted to do for some time but had never found the moment for, or the energy. Like throwing out some plants that were already old and wilting. Here in the tropics there's a plant, a kind of mountain fern, that's hard to keep nice; it never quite dies and it gets ugly and that's that, and you feel reluctant to throw it out because it's not completely dead but it's in bad shape and it depresses you, until one day you can't stand it any longer and you throw it out. What a relief! For a few cents you buy a new one and then a youthfulness enters the house.

· You have to throw out that one there in the window, it's the same way, wilting.

· But I never find the moment. No! I'm not going to throw it out until I get a new one that I really like from the nursery. So this Silvia spent those days full of energy for everything, and very intrigued, because she didn't know what there was about him that had this effect on her. Finally the day arrived, and in the morning, at the precise hour they had decided, he called. But—hold on to your hat—it was to say that he couldn't go, because he was finishing work very late that night. She pretended it wasn't important, and that's when he used the tone of voice that had struck her so before.

· What tone?

· I'll come back to that. But let's not lose the thread. Up until then it had been his eyes that had brought back the memories and stirred everything up in her. Now it was also his voice. He told her that they definitely had to find another day in the week to see each other, and he suggested Thursday. And she couldn't, not because she wanted to make herself hard to get; she really couldn't, but she said to him that he could call her on Thursday, just in case the last patient decided to cancel. Either way, she added that she was free on Saturday afternoon. But as soon as she said it she regretted it, because Saturday sounded bad. Saturday is the day when people in love have dates, it always sounds suspicious.

· It's not a day just for conversation, you're right. I like to do something more important on Saturday, begin some difficult sewing, turn a coat inside out, start a complicated embroidery, or go on a difficult visit—to someone who's sick and needs pepping up, though you know there's no cure. Or you offer condolences. Saturday is the day I feel I have more energy to do something really demanding.

· It was the only day your husband was home and spent time with the kids, and on top of that there'd always be some visitor coming around. That's probably why.

· What a good memory you have. A pity you can't use it for something more useful.

· That's not a nice thing to say, Nidia. At least I don't go around trying to make people feel sorry for me, especially my children. It must be because of the exercise I do; it's good for the circulation and makes the blood flow better to the brain.

· On Sundays Pepe would go to the game, the afternoon was easier. But Saturdays I had to look after him and the kids, and whoever came to visit too. Look after everybody and make sure they were all satisfied. They almost always were satisfied, Luci. When visitors came I always had a reserve of those little imported cookies in a tin, those English cookies. When everything from Europe was so cheap.

· Before the war.

· That I don't remember. But I'd give the kids permission to play after school; they'd have to do their homework on Sunday mornings, while Pepe slept. The main thing was not to have any fights on Saturday. And I'd always make something special for the kids, not just bread and butter to go with their steamed milk and coffee. It would be scones, or a sponge cake, or French toast if I had stale bread left over.

· Nidia, just this minute I feel a yen for some bread pudding.

· Luci, how happy we were then and we didn't even know it.

· They were good years and you lived them. They can't take that away from you, as the saying goes.

· Luci, if it stops raining today let's go to that shoe store again, come on.

· The man said they were getting in the same style in brown, but not until next week.

· . . .

· Nidia, don't start in. Good memories should help people to live, don't get sad.

· Luci, the sadness comes from inside me, it's stronger than me.

· Think of those women who never had anything in life, who never married, who didn't have children.

· Luci, tell me more about that girl.

· Okay, but I don't remember where we were.

· That she was very forward and asked to get together with him Saturday night.

· No, Nidia, she didn't say night. She said Saturday, but in the afternoon. And she didn't go that Monday or Tuesday to the art opening; it didn't matter at all to her. She wasn't going to go all the way downtown during rush hour to see an art show she didn't care about. If he was going to go, that was something else again. But she was very angry, even though he'd shown interest in seeing her again. She regretted not having canceled her last patient on Thursday right then and there and made a definite date with him, since the man could go on Thursday. She always complains about that, about not having quick reflexes; she doesn't think of things until the right moment for them has passed. With her patients that doesn't matter, because the patient is the one doing the talking and she listens. She only opens her mouth when she has something clear to say. The point is, the days dragged on but

Thursday eventually came along, and she kept hoping the last patient would cancel but no one called all day. When she sees patients she usually puts the answering machine on, but that day she disconnected it between patients so she could answer it personally, and early in the afternoon one of her patients came late, so she went downstairs to see if the doorman had received the day's mail. Which was silly because her son never writes to her. The doorman wasn't downstairs and she went out on the sidewalk looking for him. Then she heard the phone ring—you can hear it from the ground floor. And she ran up the two flights of stairs like a bat out of hell, but when she got there it stopped. Could it have been him? It was Thursday and the very hour when it might well have been him. Of course it was him, she thought. And she wanted to knock her head against the wall for having gone downstairs to look for the mail at precisely that moment. If the doorman had been at his station it wouldn't have happened, but the poor devil had chosen just that moment to go down to the basement, or who knows where, and that did it. Fortunately her patient immediately arrived and distracted her. This Silvia says that if her patients only knew, they wouldn't pay her, she'd have to pay them, because she likes this work, it relieves her nerves; she does badly if she doesn't have that grounding. And that night she was able to sleep, the situation wasn't so bad. Thursday had been more like a remote possibility, but what did matter was the call on Saturday, which was supposed to be in the morning, or noon at the latest. She always has a pile of things to do on Saturday. In earlier days, when her son was in Rio, she'd take him shopping for clothes; now she goes out to buy herself something. But that morning she canceled all her errands and waited for the call. It got to be ten, eleven, twelve noon. Nothing. It was a beautiful sunny day, and being a block away from the beach as we are, you always feel tempted to go even for just a short while. But she stayed there waiting. She tried to control her nerves and eat a little something.

· And her son, had he already gone to Mexico?

· Yes, that was last year. He went for good, to study and work, it must be over a year ago.

· Before she got sick?

· Yes, before.

· Then, Luci, that's why the poor thing got sick.

· That's when she called me on the phone to say that I should come over and talk. I was surprised, because all she ever wants to do is to leave the house; she's usually stuck inside the whole day with her patients. And she always comes here to talk, she never calls to ask me over. So I asked her what was the matter, and she said she didn't want to explain it on the phone. Well, you can imagine why: she didn't want to tie up the line. I went and found her very shaken but lively, she was all right and said she couldn't go out because she was waiting for a call. She didn't say from whom. It was around three in the afternoon so we had coffee, and after a while she served some delicious cookies, but they were a bit dry and so she brought out a little wine. She never drinks, but she drank down two glasses in a row. I noticed she was getting strange, asking me questions, and I answered her, jumping from one matter to another. She couldn't concentrate on what I was saying but kept glancing around as if she were looking for something, not me, of course. And if there was a silence she'd come out with another question. I began to feel as if she were treating me like a patient, but badly, without much interest in what I was saying, because she had this glazed look in her eyes, looking everywhere but finding nothing, of course. She has the habit of running her hand through her hair and messing it up. But she knows that, and after a while she gets up and goes to the mirror to straighten her hair. But that day she didn't, she looked bad; the circles under her eyes got darker by the minute. And then the telephone rang. She jumped as if a nerve had been pricked with a pin, and ran to the telephone but let it ring once again; why, I don't know, probably to show that she wasn't standing right there waiting for the call. It was a wrong number, which happens here in Rio all the time, as no doubt you've noticed. At five I went home; she hadn't said a word to me, but of course I realized something was going on.

· The man didn't call.

· No. At nine-thirty that night she called me. I was already watching the movie I'd rented at the video club, I don't remember which one. I was alone, of course, at that hour. And she came over, so naturally I stopped the movie. She asked if I had another one we could watch. I told her I didn't. She wanted to see a very sad one that night, she said she felt like crying. She suggested taking a taxi to check out another movie; we'd have to hurry because the club closes at ten. I didn't know that on weekends it closes at midnight. She immediately called the radio-taxi, very expensive, and we rushed over and brought back . . . I don't remember too well, it was either *Lady Hamilton* or *Waterloo Bridge*, with Vivien Leigh it was. Very sad.

· Both are sad?

· Very. Since we liked the one so much, the next day we rented the other. But I don't remember which was the first of the two.

· I'd like to see them again, I can barely remember them.

· You'll cry, do you think that's good for you? Won't crying be bad for you? This Silvia was very impressed by Vivien Leigh, especially in *Waterloo Bridge*, such a pretty girl, in her early twenties, but there's an overwhelming darkness inside her at the moments when fate gets in her way. As a psychologist, she was very impressed because Vivien Leigh made those movies when she had everything in life, so how could she know that life, if it chooses, can take everything from you, just like that? There are times when she seems to be peering into a deep well, or some bottomless precipice that has unexpectedly cracked open at her feet.

· This comes out in the movie?

· No, it's what she conveys to you as her state of mind, that what she's seeing is a bottomless well, or a black cloud covering everything in sight, the house, the kids, the husband, so that she can't see them anymore.

· But she never gets married in *Waterloo Bridge;* she dies a single woman.

· I know, but in a manner of speaking that's what she seems to be feeling, or what some people feel as they watch her: alone, faced with a black cloud, not knowing if you should try to find your home in that cloud again, with all the things that you've lost, to find your kids, who have grown up and don't need you anymore, and your husband who once kept that house solidly in place, as if he were nailing it fast to the ground with his firm step. But the man who was once so strong isn't there anymore, and if you take a step into that darkness perhaps luck will help you find the lost things, who knows? Maybe the storm that passed didn't carry the house away, as everybody thought it would. But in the movie she sees that cloud as a threat, it terrifies her, and years later in real life she lost her health, forever, and lived out the rest of her years suffering from nervous problems, and she died young, around fifty.

· When I was young I never imagined all that could happen to us, did you?

· No, I don't think so, Nidia.

· And losing my daughter, I never thought that would happen, not even in my worst dreams.

· I didn't think so many horrible things would come to pass either.

· It's because we've reached this age, Luci, and we've had time to see a lot.

· I wouldn't go into that dark cloud.

· Don't think of those things, Luci.

· If you try to make your way in the dark I don't believe you find anything, you can't even see where you're stepping, much less your own feet. Or hands.

· Luci, your two children are healthy, please don't go inventing things. Reality is enough as it is.

· It's just that I remembered all the comments this Silvia made as we watched the movies. In one there's a woman from history, Lady Hamilton, very different, carefree, but although destiny is against her, every time something contrary happens she refuses to give in, she almost can't believe she's the one going through hard times. Finally she does give in, and she ends up like a zombie in her last years; she isn't even interested in eating. She's at the end of her rope, and when she manages to steal a bottle of wine she begins to remember the good things that happened in her life, but it seems to her as if all

of it happened to another woman; she can no longer believe
all that happiness had once been hers.

· The moments when life smiled upon her.

· She thinks it all happened to someone else.

· And did this girl cry much when she saw the movie that
Saturday?

· She cried a little. And she says it did her good. Although
I think what did her good was to tell me all about it. It was
the first time she told me what was happening to her. Afterward she told me again I don't know how many times, trying
to understand why he had avoided her. Everything I just told
you.

· And on Sunday what happened?

· She decided to go spend the day at a beach two hours
from here, so as not to just be sitting by the telephone; that
had exhausted her, a whole day waiting for his call. But she
left the answering machine on, which she usually doesn't do
on holidays, or else patients will leave her messages. They're
always leaving urgent messages because they get depressed
on weekends, you should hear the stories.

· And on Monday?

· On weekdays she does connect the machine, so at the
end of the day when she listened to the tape there were two
calls but no messages. The caller had hung up without saying
anything.

· They could be a wrong number; that happens all the time
here.

· But you're always left with the doubt. I don't know if it
was Tuesday or Wednesday when she asked me to do her a
big favor: whether I could go to her house in the moments I
had nothing to do and answer the telephone while she worked,
so that the man would have to introduce himself if he called.
I went because she looked so anxious, really. They were beautiful sunny days, but I went all the same every day that week—
three days, I think. I got up earlier to go to the gym class at
the club at seven. And at nine there I was, like a soldier on
duty. I like to keep busy, you know. But the man didn't call.
And the following Saturday she didn't know whether to stay

home waiting for the miracle or not. She stayed, she couldn't resist, but she asked me to come keep her company.

· You still haven't explained what impressed her so much about the man's voice.

· That Saturday she was much calmer. Almost happy. The whole thing had become a pleasant surprise—she had thought it would never again happen in her life, getting excited that way about a man. And now she wanted to know why. She felt like a teenager.

· Tell me about his voice.

· The first thing that struck her was the look in his eyes, but that leads into something else and I don't want to lose the thread. The thing about the voice she understood right away. According to her, it was, well, she told me so many times, she explained it to me a million times, and each time in different words because I didn't quite grasp what she was saying. But for you I'll make a long story short . . .

· Yes . . .

· How can I explain it?

· Something in his voice trembled, that you told me.

· It seemed as if something inside his chest . . .

· It's just sadness, Luci. Like all of us who have lost someone.

· According to her, something strange remained inside his chest which time hadn't altered. He himself had matured, gotten a little older, but inside he continued to carry what he was before, a young boy who wasn't allowed to speak. The young boy stands quietly in a corner, doing penance, time passes and the poor thing is still there, forgotten, but he doesn't age; in his heart he remains a boy doing penance, no longer daring to open his mouth or to complain about anything. But she felt it, that he was there, a handsome boy, strong like him but without the belly, neglected by everyone, and it was to him she spoke. The boy almost didn't dare answer her; that's why his voice came out that way, hoarse, in fits and starts, because he couldn't believe that finally somebody was addressing him. You understand what I'm driving at?

· Yes, of course, but why didn't you understand her if it's so simple?

· Well, because she told it to me in many other ways. Apparently they do a lot of that with their patients, explaining things, feelings, in different ways. There's a name they have for that.

· And why didn't you understand her?

· I finally understood her, Nidia. It's called something having to do with images, a play of images or something like that. Another thing she said to me I'll tell you: that it was like the voice of someone who has fallen into a very deep well; somebody outside hears him and answers, but the one down in the well doesn't know if help will arrive in time to get him out. His wife has already vanished forever into the well's darkness, thousands of feet deep, like the mouth of an abandoned coal mine, or worse, an underground cavern where the water drags you down. He's really not asking for help, because he no longer believes he can be saved, and he says that to the person listening to him, to please not give him any hope if there's no certainty the rescue team will arrive in time.

· But what this woman wants is to save him all on her own, never mind the rescue team.

· I think she wanted to assure him that salvation was at hand, whether with her alone or with the help of others; what mattered was that he shouldn't release his grasp, he shouldn't slip even farther, because those who knew the underground cavern that lay below said he was out of danger—groping, perhaps, but away from that fatal current of freezing water which had carried his wife away. According to this Silvia, she had perceived all this in the café, but when he called her that last time on the telephone she felt again that he was in danger, that things had gotten worse.

· Poor thing, he was sad but not in danger. She invents a lot, I think.

· She figured that the poor man didn't believe that of all the people needing help she had chosen to rescue him from that cold dark cavern. You understand?

· I don't know what to say . . .

· I'd never seen her so out of control, and I've known her for six years. She's normally so restrained. When she was sick she didn't say a word to me, and that was a similar scare. I found out only afterward, when all the tests were negative and she had that sudden fit of joy.

· What fit of joy?

· That was the first time I saw her in a state of excitement, or rather, entirely out of control. She couldn't believe that she was saved, she was happy she could continue sending money to her son, for his studies. And she promised she'd never again take nonsense seriously, that she was going to enjoy life. She brought me a huge bouquet of flowers, wildflowers they were, and asked me to have her over for a drink after she was through with the patients, which was finally so late that I was already watching a movie.

· She always chooses the movie for you?

· Yes.

· Isn't that a bit overbearing?

· No, Nidia, she has very little free time. If I want I can see two or three movies a day; I have time on my hands. That day she picked a horror film, she loves those. I don't like to see them at night, because they scare me, but since it was such a special day I agreed.

· She's all whims, then.

· No, Nidia, it was a unique moment in her life, don't you understand?

· Tell me the truth, Luci, she thought she had cancer, right?

· Yes, I didn't want to say anything that might remind you of Emilsen.

· Not for a single moment can I forget Emilsen. Sometimes at night I dream she's alive, and I'm relieved; I always dream the same thing, that she's given me a false scare with the disease and it turns out not to be serious. Then I wake up and the first thing I realize is that, that she *is* dead. And each time I have to get used to the idea all over again, and it gets harder and harder.

· It's such a strange thing, that some are saved and others aren't. Who decides that? Nobody, it's a lottery. But that's how it was, this one had the worst symptoms, a malignant tumor in the womb. And she came out of it perfectly well. It was easily removed, and the spreading that was there at the beginning turned out to be nothing. I think it's something they invented so they can do a second operation, you know these doctors. To get more money out of you.

· She was lucky. And the man's wife had that illness too?

· Yes. That clinic specializes in it. They're all set up for chemotherapy and such.

· And had she spoken about the man when she was still in treatment?

· Of course not! The first time was the night of the sad movie with Vivien Leigh.

· When was all that?

· At the end of winter, some three or four months ago.

· And when did he call again?

· He didn't call; she waited a week and then decided to start looking for him. All she knew was the name of the company he'd done the transaction for at the consulate. Because in the telephone directory she didn't find anybody with his name.

· I can't believe it! So he never gave her his telephone number!

· No.

· It's because he saw it coming, he knew she was a sticky one!

· He told her something, that he was never at home, something like that. So then she called that place; it was an office, some fruit importing business. And then her calvary began, because he'd already finished his work there and nobody had his number. One of the secretaries promised to find out for her, but a day or two went by without any call from her. Then Silvia called again and had a stroke of luck. The first secretary was on her lunch break, and another one answered who did know a number where to reach him. This Silvia almost fainted; she called immediately but it was simply one of those numbers you call to leave a message. And since his name is so common, Ferreira, nobody could find him easily. It's written with *i*, not *y* as in Argentina, and on top of that they don't even pronounce the *i*, they say Ferrera, they're crazy. So she called again after the weekend, because I think that was a Friday, and on Monday they did have some real information—they gave her

the number where he was working at the time. She called
there immediately and it was a public office, in the Ministry
of Finance, and they began to pass her from one extension to
the next. But nothing. Still, at least she had left the message
on that other telephone. That calmed her down a bit, and she
waited for a few days. The next Friday she couldn't wait any
longer and called the ministry again. They passed her from
one line to the next again and put her on with someone who
apparently knew a Ferreira who did the bookkeeping. The
man came to the phone, and it turns out he did know him.
And she almost fell over because this man said to her, "Oh,
you're the lady from the Leblon neighborhood, didn't he call
you?" It came as such a surprise that she didn't dare ask
anything further; she barely managed to leave him an urgent
message to call. Nothing. A few more days went by. But
everything was getting better; he remembered her and had
even mentioned her to a friend at work.

· "I don't know how to get rid of her," he must have said.

· Her name had been on his lips, and that left a big impression on her, "the lady from Leblon." By then I didn't go over
anymore to answer her phone, because she no longer asked
me to, though I'm sure she wanted to. But that would have
been overdoing it, right?

· You bet.

· Oh, I forgot an important detail! A business trip was
coming up for her, more than ten days out of Rio. And if he
didn't call her before, imagine what a mess; he might call her
when she wasn't there, and then forget her forever.

· Go on.

· She barely managed to wait a few more days before
deciding to call the ministry again; she asked to speak to that
last man, whose name I don't remember. After going through
thousands of extensions she didn't get him, but she left him,
that last one, a message! And that man called her back and
said he hadn't seen him again but that Ferreira had to come
back there again, and he himself was a little worried also
because Ferreira had seemed very depressed some two weeks
before, that is, at the time of the famous cocktail party. This
woman almost dies right then and there; she wants to fly there

and save him from God knows what, already imagining him
on the verge of suicide; she wants to keep watch there at the
ministry from morning to night, but that would've been useless
because who knew when he would show up at that office? That
night she came over, I think it was the time we saw the other
Vivien Leigh movie. The next day she couldn't restrain herself
and called the ministry again. As always, she had to go from
one telephone operator to the next, through the thousands of
extensions they have there, and that day she called the number
the last man had given her—one of the toughest because it
was always busy. She called and this time somebody answered
immediately; she asked to speak with the last man, but the
voice that answered sounded familiar: "Is that you, Silvia?"

· I can't believe it.

· She almost fainted on the spot—he himself had answered! Not the other one but him. Out of all the thousands
of lines in that ministry. And immediately he said that they
had to get together, and she said yes and he asked for her
address. The next day was Saturday, and he said the morning
would be a good time, at ten. She couldn't believe it. She got
up early, around seven, but suddenly she felt very negative
and didn't fix up either the house or herself; she was convinced
that at the last moment he would call to cancel, saying that
something had come up. But around twenty to ten the phone
still hadn't rung, so she called me to ring her and find out if
the telephone was working. I did, and it was working perfectly. So then she combed her hair a little, but that's all, she
really didn't have the energy for anything else, she was exhausted from having fought so hard for that encounter to take
place. She started writing a letter to a girlfriend in Buenos
Aires with whom she hadn't communicated in ages, so as not
to be sitting there watching the clock. At ten o'clock sharp
the doorbell rang. She stuck her eye against the peephole,
certain that it was the doorman bringing up her gas or electricity bill or something like that. No, it was him, believe it
or not. There he was, waiting for her to open up.

4

· You're putting the light out already?

· Yes, I'm sleepy.

· You're lucky that you can sleep without having to read first.

· The walk tired me out; what a beautiful day it was. Goodnight, Luci.

· I'm going to read a little, till the pill takes effect.

· Ciao.

· Goodnight.

· But haven't you already read the whole newspaper?

· These are some old supplements; I must have kept them because there were some things left to read.

· Ciao, Luci.

· I just looked through them and I don't know why I kept them.

IMPERIAL RANCH—COLONIAL ARCHITECTURE MAY LOSE
ONE OF ITS MOST BEAUTIFUL MONUMENTS
Forty kilometers from the city of San Sebastian de Rio de Janeiro,

in the town of Santa Cruz, one of the few remnants of colonial architecture progressively deteriorates in a state of abandonment initiated almost ten years ago and accelerated now by yet another fire. The building is as remote from the government's central offices as from any intention to preserve it through public initiative. The neighbors fear that it will soon be demolished. Of the old manor that belonged to His Majesty John VI, and which later would house the first national conservatory of music, only ruins remain, to the dismay of the inhabitants of the area who wanted to see it used as a cultural center. The patio of the building has been invaded by underbrush, but the edifice itself remained practically intact until approximately two years ago, when it was seriously damaged by the first fire. Even so, the structure of the imposing two-story mansion, with its tall columns, endured until nearly two weeks ago, when a new fire consumed the columns and the roof, which is now completely destroyed. Local inhabitants presume that the fire was caused by beggars occupying the place, since after the calamity they were not sighted again. An actual visit to the manor house would be hazardous since part of the second floor—made of Riga pine—has already collapsed and tiles continue to fall, as do splinters of glass from the windows, and beams. The façade, however, seems to remain solid, due to the strength of the material used in its construction, fueling the hopes of those who support its preservation.

WAVES OF SUMMER—SEASON BEGINS WITH NEW ROCK, FILM AND TV SERIES
After the New Year's hangover, it's time to wake up to the new faces of the new Brazil. Summer is already spouting fire, especially for lovers of rock and film. And television is promising at least one exciting new series. It won't be a succession of fleeting explosions like the schizophrenic year that just passed—and by the way, there will be little room for mediocrity. With the economy down, anything that survives will have to be good.

To begin with, words like *performance pieces*, *postmodern*, *clean* and *dark* will be thrown without ceremony into the garbage pail of history. The *performance pieces* sank in the mire of their own inadequacy and lack of novelty. As to *postmodernism*, those who are ready to be dazzled can kiss all hope goodbye reading *All That Is Solid Melts into Air* by Marshall Berman, a book that deserves more than any other to be the *must* of the summer, even if only to awaken impassioned criticism. *Clean*, as was foreseen, will last only as a brand of detergent on supermarket shelves. And *dark*, the heavy-handed joke of '86, has degenerated into *the darks*, poor creatures who banalized the symbolism of somber tones and the nobility of tedium.

And to bury *darkism* once and for all, the discothèque Cubatao Dusk, exalted by the media as a temple of the *movement*, decided to bet on a change of image. Its disc jockeys are now fairly bursting with *afrobeat, hip-hop, soul, funk* and *reggae*, not to mention the inevitable Sioux and Bauhaus movements. During the whole month of January groups like Kingo, Mercenaries, Social Disturbances and a host of others will file through Cubatao Dusk. Don't ask us how a full band with a clamoring audience of music lovers is going to fit into that minimalist cellar. And we may as well leave the acoustics in God's hands. But since the shows don't start till midnight, fun will be guaranteed.

Stepping out of the shadows, The Flying Circus is programing a superfestival of rock with The Gross Plebeians, The Innocents and two nights of specials, one *punk* and another with new groups from Brasília. Another promise is the show put on by The Mudguards of Success, who will play on the 25th in Remo do la Lagoa Stadium, after having toured half the world. But the ones to open fire will be Kongo.

Now that rock is an integral and expressive part of popular Brazilian music, the purists of populism can cry their eyes out— the time has come for these electrified folk to strut their stuff. An avalanche of new names is coming down: from Rio the abovementioned Kongo, as well as The Fake Picassos and Jot Deduh, two expressions of tribal *funk*. And don't forget Black Future, or rather nihilism carried to its logical conclusion, and Bad Fayth, cultivators of psychedelic *rhythm 'n' blues*. From São Paolo they're announcing The Ghetto, Fall Violet and the total stupefaction of Vzyadoq Moe, while Brasília provides the brand-new groups Panic, School for Scandals, Art of Darkness, Sodomite Martian and The Male Black Women. Add to these the dozens of so far unscheduled groups and artists and we have before us a most appetizing musical menu. A detail: the names cited merely represent the tip of the iceberg.

SCIASCIA DENOUNCES CAREERISM IN STRUGGLE
WITH MAFIA, DIVIDES ITALY

Rome—The Sicilian writer Leonardo Sciascia is paying a high price for denouncing a genuine and flourishing anti-mafia industry. This industry is not limited to manufacturing respectable public figures, but also facilitates and furthers successful careers for politicians and magistrates, principally in Sicily. Sciascia fired the first shot with a full-page article published in *Corriere della Sera*, a newspaper with a great tradition in Italy. Once more he acted true to the form and style that have marked his personality and his work as a provocative, nonconformist intellectual, a demanding libertarian always drawn to difficult causes and challenging ideas.

Already recognized as the first great non-folkloric writer of postwar Italy, the austere Leonardo Sciascia, 66 years old and with 18 published works of fiction and theater behind him, was also the first to use literature with vigor and mastery as an efficient weapon against the mafioso system and methods. Without his works, it would have been difficult to obtain the information and knowledge about the mafia that awakened and mobilized the best fighters against the Cosa Nostra of our times.

. . . in the name of the uncontrollable aversion he always felt for all myths. Or inspired by his profound dislike of the symbols and manifestations of power.

. . . which brought him to write the article—once more, against the grain—that wounded and scandalized the honest people of Palermo and divided Italy into two blocs, those in favor of Sciascia and those against. As in the days of . . .

. . . life, Leonardo Sciascia again becomes the least ingratiating social critic in the country. This time the butt of Sciascia's attack is the so-called Anti-Mafioso Front, composed of magistrates, politicians and an association that designates itself the *Coordinamento dei Democratici*. The writer attacks and denounces them because they are turning into a conformist power that brooks no criticism, controls or serious analysis, that resorts to the logic of emergency procedures to insult and condemn whoever disagrees with its actions. Sciascia places under suspicion the current administrator of Palermo, a young and unorthodox Christian Democrat, and also an eminent judge . . .

. . . and to supervise effectively the city of Palermo. Sciascia sees this as nothing more than a politician's career maneuver. He would be banking on merits gained in the last six years—placing at risk even his life and that of his family—to obtain a promotion, his election to the post of . . .

. . . and since the publication of the article all of Italy has been witness to a public "lynching" of Sciascia sanctioned and carried out not only in Palermo but throughout the country, by men and organizations that should not ignore or forget the value of his good faith and his nearly thirty-year contribution toward creating a brave civic resistance to the mafia crimes that drain and demoralize Italy.

THE HOURS ACQUIRE STYLE
No better way to begin the new year than winding up the clock.
In the Rio market you have everything for every taste. There was an undeniable boom in the sale of clocks and watches. The best-selling models . . .
. . . decorative clocks were more daring this year, but those which . . .
. . . overdid it. WHAT'S IN: waterproof watches//wall clocks in granite, marble and various stones//digits to indicate each hour. WHAT'S ON THE WAY OUT: loud colors//watches as evening jewelry//chain wristbands.

CONSUMER'S PROFILE.
In the theater and on television her name is always synonymous with success. Born in the sunny region of . . .
. . . and as a consumer she doesn't deprive herself of anything. Let's take a look at her favorites.
Perfume: Several, among them Magie Noire and Azzaro ("but I also like those colognes that smell like a forest, so delicious"). *Shampoo:* Those made in São Paolo under the label Venado de Oro, for bleached hair. *Soap:* Jurúa for the face and the North American product Lint for the body. *Eyewash:* Lerin, daily applications. *Cigarets:* It's been precisely six years, eight months and ten days since she last smoked ("Thank God"). *Hair removal:* With hot wax at the Beauty Institute Garden in Copacabana ("I've been a client for 25 years"). *Hairdresser:* . . . *Deodorant:* . . . *Jeans:* . . . *Underwear:* Italian La Perla panties ("They don't leave marks, due to the silky quality of the cotton threads"); bras of any make—she always wears them; and for exercise, exclusively the North American label Exquisite Form. *Stockings:* Kendal for work on television, for the theater L'eggs and for sunny mornings in Rio the popular make Drastosa. *Analyst:* Astréa ("I've been in analysis for three and a half years, and it's improved my thinking a lot"). *Favorite director:* Woody Allen. *Consumer's dream:* "A refrigerator that never breaks down so that my caviar doesn't spoil." *Favorite saying:* "I'm not ashamed of changing my mind, because I'm not ashamed of thinking" (Schiller).

. . .

THE BAY OF THE 365 ISLANDS
Officially discovered January 6, 1502, the day of Epiphany, and
thus called Angra dos Reis ("The Kings' Anchor"), the dazzling
bay was by then already known as a recreation spot for the Tamoio
Indians. According to historical records, there they swam, went
boating, fished and massaged themselves in the waterfalls. Exactly the same program for which folks from São Paulo and Rio,
as well as tourists from everywhere 400 years later, flock to the
bay in search of its two thousand beaches.
    The rain has been persistent this year, but sooner or later the
heat is going to show us who's boss of the season here and . . .
    . . . there, around 1625, an effigy of the Holy Virgin arrived in
a sailboat, destination São Paulo. But each time the sailboat at-
tempted to continue on, the sky grew dark and a downpour began,
which, however, quickly cleared up at the very moment the vessel
touched the port of Angra, taking refuge from the storm. The
effigy seemed to have taken a liking to the place, and the people
there built a church around it.
    . . . to any of its 365 islands the first step is to look for the
Santa Luzia dock and decide between a ferry or a "flyer," speed-
boats for those in a hurry. The route to paradise—which invites
dreams of pirate adventures, sunken treasures and romantic picnics—offers stops at local bars that serve enormous shrimp, fried
fish and squid.
    . . . and on Isla Grande the charm resides in the simplicity of
one's encounter with nature and not in luxury. There are only two
hotels, with minimal comforts but lots of hospitality. No restau-
rants, but you can eat fresh fish, prepared with distinction, in
either of the two bars. And visitors to the region must either
resort to the little fishing boats or stretch their legs on long walks
through the jungle and over the rocks.
    Villa Abraham, where small boats from the mainland lay anchor,
is a calm and sleepy port with four thousand inhabitants and
modest houses, some of them dating from the colonial era. The
place is free from the roar and smoke of motors; the few auto-
mobiles belong to the adminstration and to the police. In ten
minutes on foot you can reach the first waterfall, which empties
into a natural pool with a bed of brilliant stones. Only a few yards

away is the ancient aqueduct, with crumbling blocks displaying still the most fanciful variations on the Maltese Cross, evoking images of both horror and sublime mysticism.

The aqueduct had the function of channeling water to the quarantine station, built on the beach in 1771 and today in ruins. The pavilion originally served as shelter for those arriving from Europe who had to be temporarily quarantined.

. . . a stop is compulsory, to take a dip in the Pocket of Heaven; you can see five yards down to the bottom through its crystalline water. And close by, five hundred yards away, is the Beach of the Small Congregation, where schools of *maringas*, tiny and very agile fish, are not frightened by the occasional swimmer, as on the other hand does occur with the sergeant fish, medium-sized with very pretty yellow and blue stripes. In the surrounding jungle, sparrows, blackbirds, swallows, parrots and even toucans sing. And farther on, the Beach of the Bat hovers, shady and secret, where the house built in 1629 by pirate Juan Lorenzo still stands, and in total contrast farther away the Cove of the Palms spreads open, where, surprisingly, the water and the surrounding jungle foliage are exactly the same shade of green, waters and foliage losing their boundaries as when in a dream past and present become one, or the nonexistent and the real, the horrible and the sublime, truth and lie, pain and pleasure. And yet farther on . . .

BIKINIS COME RAIN OR SHINE
Two pieces eagerly await the strong and dependable sun: the bras and panties of our modern bikinis. At the beginning of every season, designers such as Zilda Maria Costa fan the flames of creativity to reinvent those select rags that mark one of the few areas in which Brazilian fashion displays its courage.

. . . They are two little strips of Lycra fabric that are cut, sewn, tied with who knows what new knot, all to avoid looking like last year's model.

. . . If this year's model is not significantly different from last year's, those of us girls who go in for water sports, and especially body surfing, manage to reinvent the suits by tying their straps in unusual ways: we tie the bra to the briefs, we cross the straps at the shoulder and transform them into an imitation of a one-piece bathing suit.

One of the manufacturers bringing out its new collection dis-

tributed a brochure, with remarks on the research trips its designers have made in search of new ideas. "Nobody copies
anybody, but everybody copies everybody." Common to almost
all the collections, however, is the fabric Lycra, an international
product of Du Pont.

For '87–'88, tart colors are definitely in fashion: green, pink,
orange, turquoise, in clear and combined tones. And so are unexpected knots, for example those that are tied over the panties.
And demicup bras. And delta-winged briefs. And the discreet
transparencies of the cloth. And though it's hard to believe, cur-
tain-model bras remain in style.

On the other hand, the shell and stone embellishments have
been banished to the provinces, along with the tank top and all
manner of stripes and spangles, and, take note, also the problem-
atic crochetwork."

A COUNTERSTITCH FOR THE MINITANGAS
Not everything in fashion is tanga and delta-wing. Recognizably
young labels, like São Paulo's Transport and The Carioca Company, brought out bikinis with large briefs and bras to facilitate
the practice of sports and create an old-fashioned silhouette. It's
a parallel line that can be more sophisticated and satisfy those
consumers who don't accept the radical dips and dental-floss cuts.

IMPERIAL RANCH—COLONIAL ARCHITECTURE MAY LOSE ONE
OF ITS MOST BEAUTIFUL MONUMENTS.
Forty kilometers from the city of San Sebastian de Rio de Janeiro,
in the town of Santa Cruz, one of the few remnants of colonial
architecture progressively deteriorates in a state of abandonment
initiated almost ten years ago and accelerated now by yet another
fire.

. . . old manor that belonged to His Majesty John VI, and which
later would house the first national conservatory of music, only
ruins remain, to the dismay of the inhabitants of the . . .

. . . as a cultural center. The patio of the building has been
invaded by underbrush, but the edifice itself remained practically
intact until approximately two years ago, when . . .

. . . the first fire. Even so, the structure of the imposing two-
story mansion, with its tall columns, endured until nearly . . .

. . . made of Riga pine—has already collapsed and tiles continue to fall, as do splinters of glass from the windows, and beams. The façade, however, seems to remain solid, due to the strength of the material used in its construction, fueling the hopes of those who support its preservation.

THE BAY OF THE . . .

. . . to paradise—which invites dreams of pirate adventures, sunken treasures and romantic picnics—offers stops at . . .

. . . you can reach the first waterfall, which empties into a natural pool with a bed of brilliant stones. Only a few yards away is the ancient aqueduct, with crumbling . . .

. . . in the Pocket of Heaven; you can see five yards down to the bottom through its crystalline . . .

. . . of *maringas*, tiny and very agile fish, are not frightened by the occasional . . .

. . . the sergeant fish, medium-sized with very pretty yellow and blue stripes . . .

. . . surrounding jungle, sparrows, blackbirds, swallows, parrots and even toucans sing. And farther on, the Beach of the Bat hovers, shady and secret . . .

. . . pirate Juan Lorenzo . . .

. . . farther away the Cove of the Palms spreads open, where, surprisingly, the waters and the surrounding jungle foliage are exactly the same shade of green, waters and foliage losing their boundaries as when in a dream past and present become one, or the nonexistent and the real, the horrible and the sublime, truth and . . .

· Nidia, are you asleep?

· . . .

· Goodnight.

· Did you say something, Luci?

· What a blessing, that you can sleep so easily.

· Put out the light and you'll go to sleep. Think about beautiful things.

· You too.

· . . .

· But what could I think about?

· Something nice that you just read about.

· . . .

· Are you listening to me?

· Yes, but I couldn't concentrate much on what I read.

· Think that you're going to be able to sleep tranquilly the whole night long, Luci.

· I'm going to think about that, Nidia.

5

· That was quick.

· Well, she'd taken a tranquilizer and it had too strong an effect on her, so she fell asleep while we were talking.

· That woman is going to come to no good, Luci.

· Don't scare me, please.

· Deep down I feel sorry for her; why did she recover her health if she can't even take advantage of it?

· The devil put that man in her path, Nidia. But the real reason why I came back so quickly is that I was nervous, since Ñato should be calling any minute now.

· You're afraid it's going to take him longer to get here, admit it.

· What I'm afraid of is that they'll convince him to stay there.

· If Ñato is delayed I'll stay longer. I'm not going to let you stay alone.

· . . .

· How horrible it is to live in a cold country. You couldn't get used to it now.

· To go live in Lucerne at this age, I'll die in that cold. I'm already used to the heat here.

· At our age having a place where it's never winter is

priceless. You don't know how much I suffer when I return to Argentina.

· Nidia, it's incredible, with all the people who've passed through my life, the only one I have left is you.

· You should be ashamed! How about your two children?

· One lives with his wife and ten cats, thousands of miles away, and the other, even worse, is married to his career.

· God will punish you, Luci, for being so discontent.

· The only thing I ask God is that if there's another world I don't want to be left alone there. But after this life there's nothing, luckily.

· Of course there's nothing. A good thing there's no other world. There's already enough injustice in this one.

· Nidia, are there people who are luckier, or doesn't anybody get away with it?

· There are people who are a lot luckier, and not because they deserve it. Emilsen was a girl who never did any wrong to anyone, and that was her reward, to die at forty-eight without seeing her children graduate, or anything. Can we take a walk, Luci?

· Are you joking? My legs are so weak I could barely walk up the stairs to see the woman next door.

· Why is it that I can't stand being inside these four walls? Just to get out a little gives me so much relief . . .

· Today you can't get rid of that memory, right?

· Yes, of all that the poor little thing suffered, before dying, all that went on in the clinic.

· Going out relieves you a bit, right?

· Why is that?

· Let's go then, Nidia. If Ñato wants to call he'll call later.

· But put on more comfortable shoes.

· No, they all hurt.

· I'll take a jacket in case it gets cooler.

· But let's go now, the sooner we go out the sooner we'll come back.

· Stop complaining, Luci, the air will do you good.

· On the island all one could do was to take a little walk at night.

· Did you like it, or was it the kind of trip you wouldn't take again?

· It's for couples. At night there's no place to go; I got bored.

· Everybody says it's so marvelous . . . I must admit, it makes me want to go. Can we go someday, Luci?

· During the day you feel you can't possibly take in so many gorgeous natural wonders, but at night there's no electricity. Imagine.

· And according to her, there they were very happy.

· Things can be deceiving when people are on vacation. I was more interested to know how things had gone here. But she's always telling and retelling the business about the island.

· How long has it been since he called her?

· A long time.

· Poor thing, I feel sorry for her. He's not going to call her anymore.

· See, Nidia, all those armed guards are paid by private individuals. Very rich people live here, that's why you can go out at night alone.

· I know. The maid told me there are high-ranking military officers around here. At least, I think that's what she was trying to explain, but she speaks too fast for me.

· You see, that's her office window, the one with the light on.

· She's waiting for the call.

· Maybe she fell asleep from the tranquilizer, with the light on.

· . . .

· Poor Silvia, she's got it bad. But you're right, if she got her hopes up it's because she wanted to. The time he came to her house for the first and only time, it was clear there were problems. But she never wants to talk about that day.

· You couldn't squeeze the truth out of her?

· Some of it. I don't know, it might be just my impression, but something about that day, it doesn't quite add up.

· Luci, before I forget, who is that boy in the doorway at night, in front of her building?

· The night watchman.

· Just a doorman?

· Yes, he's been there for months, but they still haven't given him the uniform. A handsome boy, isn't he?

· When I saw him now I thought there was something about his eyes like the neighbor's man.

· I didn't notice.

· Luci, how could you not notice that boy's eyes?

· I don't know; there must be so many good-looking people in Rio that I'm already used to it.

· He has a very sad look in his eyes, poor kid. And he spends the whole night awake, thinking about God knows what. There must be some terrible sorrow in his life.

· But this woman here didn't say that her man had a sad look in his eyes.

· I figured he had a look like that, like this poor kid's.

· It might not be sadness; sometimes long, curved lashes give that impression . . . See, it's in his building that the high-ranking officer lives, the one the girl told you about.

· But I never saw anybody wearing a military uniform in this street.

· Nidia, even I, in all the years I've lived here, have never seen a uniform on any street.

· They must not like to be seen with their uniforms on.

· That way people don't realize what they are.

· But here they're not murderers like in Argentina, or are they?

· Much less so, it seems.

· Tell me, Luci, the neighbor's man, is he as fat as that one crossing the street up there?

· No, don't be silly. Anyway, whenever she talks about that day he went to her house, it's always about his arriving, never about his leaving.

· What you told me is that at least he arrived on time that morning. Did he bring her flowers, or did he come empty-handed?

· What could be better than bringing her all his enthusiasm? I already told you that she wasn't even made up, her hair wasn't even brushed. At least she'd washed her face. And she noticed that he looked very flustered, as if he'd been running. She asked him if he had been. And he said no, that he was just nervous because he wanted so much to see her. At that point she must have smiled, or given him some sign, perhaps without realizing it, because the man threw himself on her and didn't let go. Almost without saying a word.

· I can't believe what you're saying.

· I thought you weren't going to be shocked by anything.

· And they didn't talk at all?

· Afterward.

· Luci, I'm not shocked by anything. Tell me all the details and you'll see I don't get shocked.

· She really didn't tell me anything. Luckily she'd just taken a bath, although I already told you she had no make-up on.

· She had it all figured out. Tell me something, does she usually bathe in the morning or at night?

· When she comes home after the last patient her hair's wet.

· That's what I'm telling you. She took a bath that morning because she had it all thought out and she was more than ready. It's obvious that she's a fast operator, Luci, you just don't want to see it.

· But then why did she get so worked up over this man, if as you say she's always having affairs?

· You're the one who must know why.

· Let's take it step by step; let me tell you the story and then you'll be able to figure out why.

· Did she like him as a man?

· She didn't talk much about that. But she did say something important, and it was the opposite of what she'd experienced with the Mexican; with him she was always the one to do the touching, whereas with this one he always touched her first. That's so nice, when someone reaches out for you; it doesn't have to be a man necessarily, it can be . . . I don't know, my granddaughter when she was little would hang on to me . . . it's the most wonderful thing in the world when someone you love hangs on to you and doesn't want to let go.

· My grown-up grandchildren hug me hard, too hard. The

boys, I mean. I do like it when the little one hugs me, he's more gentle.

· The point is, the man was a little on the shy side at first, but when he threw himself at her, that was it. They stayed there awhile on a sofa, and when he began to take off her clothes she got them to move into the bedroom, where it was darker, with the curtains closed.

· From your place you can see if she closes the bedroom curtains or not. And she was closing them in the morning! Did you realize it? That time, I mean.

· Don't be silly! I don't keep an eye on her curtains, and the last thing I imagined was that she'd get to the point so quickly. Afterward I understood why it happened that way, because the two of them, she as much as he, were under a terrific nervous strain.

· But before he came in they'd never even kissed.

· Of course not. They'd spoken that one day in the consulate and later on the telephone. That was all.

· And did she enjoy intimacy with him? Look, Luci, how with old age I forget everything, but I do remember that when I was a young girl there were boys who drove me crazy because they were very tall or very handsome. Anyway, I would act like a ninny, I was so eager for them to ask me to dance, or for even the briefest rendezvous in some square. But then, when they kissed me, sometimes it would burst like a bubble, I just suddenly stopped liking them. Because their hands were sort of awkward, I don't know, or they had bad breath, or they kissed too hard. And others who appealed to you less when you just saw them in passing, they could kiss you and drive you crazy. The ones who knew how to caress. I remember that as if it were yesterday.

· We're going back sixty years or more.

· Luci, I remember it as clearly as if it were yesterday. I can feel that hand right now.

· Really?

· You won't laugh if I tell you something? A chill just ran down my back, I remembered it so vividly. Well, I won't interrupt you any further. The point is, the man knew how to conquer her in this way too, because if he hadn't she wouldn't be sitting by the telephone the way she is right now.

· But she didn't tell any details about that time. About the island she did, you'll see. Afterward he asked her for coffee, and that's when she began asking more about his life, about how his kids were, a little of everything, because her head was spinning so fast, wondering what kind of man this was, deep down.

· Was it then that he continued criticizing the poor wife?

· Oh hush, he'd done that on the telephone, but that morning he got bullheaded and didn't want to tell her a thing. For her this was unexpected, because she wanted him to talk, thirsty as she was to know everything.

· He did well; he put her in her place.

· What do you mean?

· Well, Luci, he didn't treat her as a doctor but, rather, as what she was, a stranger in whom he didn't have the slightest trust.

· I think you're right. She wasn't expecting it; she was sure he'd come there to unburden himself. So she persisted and asked him about his work, anything, about the economic situation in the country and the inflation, and how they affected him, and what his children thought about the current government, who knows, things like that, I don't remember too well now. He didn't answer anything special, because what he wanted was to listen to her.

· . . .

· She had to tell him about her life, because he didn't say a word. He was determined not to talk.

· Good for him.

· Poor Silvia, she wanted to know everything, she sincerely wanted to help. Another, more self-centered woman would have flustered him talking about herself, you see? You don't understand that about her, that she's a woman who's always ready to listen to others.

· But then she makes them pay.

· Oh, Nidia, if you dislike her that much then I'd better not tell you any more.

· You'll say she wasn't going to make him pay, not in

money, but the truth is she wanted to grab him for herself, get him in her clutches even though the man's scars hadn't even healed yet.

· Of course she wanted him for herself, that's nothing new.

· Look how beautiful the ocean is. Of course, since you have it all year round you're already tired of it.

· No, Nidia, you know very well that in the morning I love to go down to the beach. It's just that my bones don't let me go out twice a day.

· I didn't realize, we could have invited her to come walking with us, couldn't we? Because she's depressed too.

· I think she fell asleep; in any case, she wouldn't want to leave the telephone, at this hour more than ever she gets up her hopes that he's going to call.

· She doesn't know that the worst thing is to stay indoors.

· That day she had no choice but to tell him everything about her life. And she didn't dare tell him the whole truth, that she wasn't going out with anyone, that she was alone. She invented a story that she was dating a man she hadn't seen for a while, and not only him but another one. The subject came up later because he asked her what she did all day long, and she began by telling him about the morning activities first, of course. And eventually the moment came to tell him what she did at night.

· She didn't tell him the truth, but she does to you?

· I know exactly what she does, I have a clear view of her bedroom window.

· But not of her street door, or the office window, which are on the other side. You'll have to forgive me, Luci, because I know you like her, but she's hiding something.

· Do you think you know everything that happened to her? We're only just at the beginning. Basically her life is pretty routine; she gets up at seven or so, because by eight her patients start to come. Each one is forty-five minutes, with fifteen minutes of rest in between. All that time she pays the closest attention, trying to pinpoint each one's problems. Then she has lunch around one, rests a little, and back at three o'clock again till seven and sometimes eight.

· She earns a good living, then.

· And she pays whatever she wants in taxes, because she works independently. In very few years' time she's bought not only the apartment she lives in but others to rent out. The truth is, she doesn't know what to do with all the money she makes. And two afternoons a week she doesn't see patients, so that she can study; she's always keeping up with the field. One of those afternoons she spends alone reading, and the other free afternoon she meets with a group of psychologists to discuss things. So basically she never stops.

· And her son?

· The kid's not easy; he doesn't seem to know what he wants yet, but he's studying graphic design there. Here he was studying something else. He's nineteen.

· I remember when Baby was nineteen. It was his first year at the university. He'd get up at five to study. And I'd get up with him, to brew his maté.

· Before she . . . when they were just back from Mexico, she'd stay home every night with the kid; they'd have dinner together and afterward he'd want to watch a little television and she couldn't go out much. But now the kid's not there, night or day. And the worst part, I didn't tell you, is that he doesn't even want to come home for vacations; he has all his friends there, you know what I mean. It's a good thing she's busy all day long, because when eight o'clock in the evening comes along she's as lonely as a dog.

· Why do they say that, "lonely as a dog"? Most dogs have someone to take care of them.

· These shoes don't hurt much, thank goodness. One thing, Nidia: when you talk about your son to her, don't say Baby.

· It comes out that way. We've always said Baby.

· A man who's over fifty years old, calling him Baby . . .

· I think we should have called her, invited her for a walk.

· No, Nidia, don't stop now, turning back is something I just won't do.

· Yes, let's call her; I feel sorry for her sometimes. Other times she makes me angry.

· No, Nidia, I'm not turning back, that's too much walking.

· Another day, then . . . Look, some night when it's

warmer we could have a beer together at one of those tables.

· But it's not good for the blood pressure.

· There are always people in that bar; it must make a fortune.

· It's a very popular spot in Rio. They come from all over to sit there, have a beer, and look at the sea.

· Do you think it will be too cold if we sit and have one today?

· Yes, Nidia, don't be tempted. Walking it's pleasant but sitting still we'll get cold.

· What freedom, those girls alone at night.

· Times certainly have changed.

· Luci, these are probably just like the girls in Argentina, or worse. They won't stop at a few kisses in the doorway.

· They begin so young, Nidia. In my building there were some who were mere babies just a few years ago, and from one day to the next I saw them get all made up to go out at night. And they looked different, like women who knew everything about life. But then I saw them again when they went off to school without makeup on, and they still looked like children. Except there was a shadow in their faces, as if they were already weighed down by some disappointment.

· And so they get passed around. If it doesn't matter to men that women are like that now, it's not a problem anymore. But things were nicer before.

· I don't know, Nidia. If you were lucky enough to get a good husband, then things were nicer. Just a matter of luck.

· I'm more and more convinced of that. What you deserve doesn't mean a thing. Look at that girl, what a pretty face.

· An angel, isn't she?

· The boy is adorable too.

· What youth there is in this city, Nidia, it's enough to leave you speechless.

· Look, they're getting into a car now, Luci.

· With that fire the young have inside, and without a mother to hold her back, who's going to keep that girl from getting into trouble?

· I feel like going over and speaking to her, Luci. A girl who has everything, taking the risk that tomorrow may be her first day of suffering. It's terrible to fall for somebody and then lose him. How can that poor girl know what life might have in store for her?

· Around any corner, as the old women used to say, Nidia.

· As girls we'd laugh at those things, but now we know it's true.

· Who knows where they're going. Even if you wanted to . . . you couldn't stop her; she wouldn't listen to you. I hope he's not important to her, that it's not true love. Because, modern as women may be, they're always more foolish than men, I think; they become more easily attached. And once she's attached, she's had it; if she loses him it'll cost her plenty of tears. Though if she's as young as that she must still have her parents, and her whole life ahead of her to forget.

· And so many other boys. Oh well, I wish her luck.

· But did you see how fast they took off? How crazy they are to speed like that.

· Your neighbor hadn't had a suitor for a long time?

· That's why she felt ashamed, so to make herself seem more desirable she told him that she was going out with the two beaux from before. I know them; one was an Argentine sales representative for some chemical product, who lives here but travels a lot around the country. He's divorced, with his whole family in Buenos Aires, but she says she got fed up because he's a very superficial man who couldn't talk about anything. She didn't want to see him anymore.

· And the other one?

· You're going to be shocked.

· It all depends. You're the one who's always shocked.

· It was long ago, when she had just arrived in Rio de Janeiro, and she went swimming in the ocean, here at the beach in Leblon, not realizing how dangerous it was. One day as she was swimming a treacherous current dragged her out and a strong young man helped her return to shore; she couldn't do it alone. That was some years ago when she was around forty, which is to say yes, he was much younger.

· And she set her sights on that one too?

· No, on the contrary. The boy was a bit of a lost soul; he was the one who was really drowning, and she was the life-

saver. Anyway, at that time I didn't know her very well, so
I didn't follow the thing too closely. She helped him a little,
gave him some therapy without charging him, as a way of
returning the favor, but she says that it didn't work at all,
because the boy wanted another kind of relationship and that's
the worst thing for these treatments. Besides, she felt
ashamed because of her son.

· But did they have an affair or not?

· No, he pushed for it but she never consented. At any
rate, she told this man—Ferreira, who goes by the name Zé,
short for José—that morning she told him that she was still
going out with those two men, so as not to give the impression
that she was a discarded piece of furniture.

· But in reality she doesn't see them anymore. Or so she
says.

· If only she did, then she wouldn't be so alone.

· . . .

· Nidia, did you ever find out if Luisita Brenna got better?

· No, there's no way she's going to get better.

· In your letters you never answered me on that. Did you
call her for me?

· Oh, Luci.

· What?

· I didn't want to tell you.

· No, Nidia . . . don't tell me.

· Almost a year ago.

· She was my last remaining classmate from the university, out of all those girls.

· Really?

· One by one they've all joined the parade.

· It's just that few reach eighty; we should be grateful to
have reached this age, shouldn't we?

· I'd always go with her after an evening class and we'd
pass the bar on the corner of Talcahuano and Tucumán, where
this boy who drove her wild was always sitting. In good
weather the tables were out on the sidewalk, but in the cold,
facing that big open Lavalle Square, all you could see were
the tables next to the window and the faces behind the fogged-
up panes of glass. And in the end nothing happened; the boy

would look at her and look at her, never at me, but he never
spoke to her. Years later he married a really rich girl from
the provinces. And poor Luisita lost years waiting for him
until that other one whom she married showed up. Oh, Nidia,
now it's me getting a chill, one just ran down my spine, remembering that bar as if it were yesterday, and those boys
with their hair slicked back with brilliantine. They too must
all be dead by now. But I'm seeing them just as they were,
some of them very handsome; there were two types, remember? The slick ones, and the Bohemians with long hair and no
brilliantine, parted down the middle. Each one with his particular charm.

· They were sort of wan, very different from the ones
here.

· Sometimes the glass was so fogged up that you couldn't
see anything, and it made you wish you could get closer and
wipe the window with your hand to see better. But we never
dared.

· That bar on Talcahuano and Tucumán is still there.

· And the talk was the best part. There wasn't one of
them who didn't know some poem by heart, and at some moment they'd recite it. Of course, there would always be some
fellow who had actually written what he recited, and that
would bomb. But if they stuck to the classics it all ran fine.

· Do you remember any of those?

· *"Hush, Princess, hush, says her fairy godmother; he's
riding this way on his wingèd horse . . ."* How did it go? Something about the joyous knight who adores you unseen . . . I
don't remember any more, Nidia. Wait a second, it'll come
back. Wait . . . *"The joyous knight who adores you unseen,
and who comes from far off, having conquered Death, to kindle
your lips with a kiss of true love!"*

· Try to remember. It's the poem about the little princess,
right?

· It was very famous.

· Try and remember.

· *"Alas, the poor Princess, whose mouth is a rose, would
be a swallow or a butterfly . . ."* But I don't remember what
comes next, Nidia. Wait . . . *"And the flowers are sad for the*

flower of the court: the jasmines of the east . . ." Oh, I don't remember!

· I wouldn't remember a single word.

· "*. . . the dahlias from the west, and the roses from the south. The poor little Princess with the wide blue eyes is imprisoned in her gold, imprisoned in her tulle, in the marble cage of the royal palace . . .*" But I don't know what comes next . . .

· Try and remember, Luci.

· "*Oh to fly to the land where there is a prince—(The Princess is sad. The Princess is pale.)—more brilliant than daybreak, more handsome than April! 'Hush, Princess, hush,' says her fairy godmother, 'he's riding this way on his wingèd horse. . .'* " And I'm lost again.

· "*Hush, Princess, hush, says her fairy godmother . . .*" And what else?

· "*Hush, Princess, hush, says her fairy godmother . . . says her fairy godmother . . .*"

· Go on, Luci.

· Oh, how did it go? I already said it . . .

· Something about the horse . . .

· Yes, the wingèd horse . . . what comes next? "*The joyous knight who adores you unseen, and who comes from far off, having conquered Death, to kindle your lips with a kiss of true love!*"

· Luci, you are really something! That very same poem was recited to me by someone, but I can't remember his face anymore. I can hear the voice as clear as a bell! As if it were right now, but not the foggiest memory of the face! You were amazing to remember that particular poem.

· Well, it was the most popular one then, Rubén Darío's "Sonatina."

· Luci, wait a minute, I want to rest a minute, against this palm tree.

· What's wrong?

· My legs suddenly felt weak. I'll be all right in a minute.

· Nidia . . . are you feeling bad?

· I'd like so much to remember the boy's face. Especially his eyes.

· At least you remembered the voice.

· It seems to me that I've never heard that voice again, or even thought of it, in all this time. Could it have been around 1925?

· More or less.

· Then almost seventy years have passed.

· Nidia, you're acting senile! Please don't add more years than there already are, from twenty-five to eighty-seven it's sixty-two years.

· That's almost the same; it's not such a big difference, so you don't have to call me senile. Sometimes you're too brutal, Luci.

· What was the voice like?

· What voice?

· The voice of the boy who recited "Sonatina" to you.

· No, it wasn't like the voice of the neighbor's man.

· What does one thing have to do with the other?

· It was the voice of a young boy, a dreamer. But one who dreams of beautiful things only. And who expects the best out of life.

·   . . .

· Luci, tell me about the island.

· About my trip?

· No, about when those two went. Tell me everything.

· My feet are starting to hurt. Let's go home so I can take off my shoes and tell you the whole thing.

6

· Now your feet must really hurt.

· Those stairs are tough, to do them twice in a row. But I'm all set with my reading for the night.

· Let me see what it is.

· It's the biography of Vivien Leigh. I already told you. But it's in Portuguese, if not you could read it too.

· You didn't have anything else to read tonight?

· It's just that I'd been waiting quite a while for her to finish it and lend it to me. She sent me flying back home just in case the phone rang. It didn't ring, did it?

· . . .

· Did it ring?

· No.

· Why didn't you answer me right away? She's going crazy over this business; that's why she sent us the night watchman.

· Back in Buenos Aires when your phone breaks down it takes months for them to fix it for you.

· Oh, now my feet really do hurt. On top of the walk, coming up these stairs.

· But there was no need to make you come up; if the telephone wasn't working the man couldn't call her; what could she lose by coming down here?

· No, she asked the night watchman to let her know when

he saw us pass by, but the kid misunderstood and told us to go upstairs.

· Did her man ever call here?

· No, but she gave him my telephone number. That's why she hopes that if he can't reach her directly he'll call here.

· That woman's crazy.

· It's love, Nidia. Plain and simple.

· Poor thing. The truth is, she's making me feel sorry for her.

· Oh, how they hurt. I shouldn't have gone up the second time.

· You could have waited till tomorrow for the damn book.

· I had it in my hands the first time I went up; I don't know why I put it down afterward. She was so nervous that she made me nervous, wanting me to go home right away just in case the telephone rang.

· Luci, the phone did ring.

· When?

· Now, when you went up the second time, to get the book.

· And who was it?

· When I got there it stopped ringing.

· Did you take long to get to it?

· No.

· Are you sure?

· Yes. And don't go picking up the book now, because we'd agreed that you'd tell me all about the island.

· It couldn't have been Ñato; he lets the phone ring a long time.

· Besides, Luci, at this hour in Switzerland it's around three in the morning.

· My back hurts, Nidia.

· You talk while I put on the water for the camomile.

· You get there in a boat that leaves every morning from some seedy port, two hours from here by car. There's just that one boat a day. It was a psychologists' congress about goodness knows what, a conference about . . . oh, something like the psychology of the masses. Some left-wing thing, you know. Without funding from any government. He had flatly

refused but then at the last minute accepted. Each participant
paid for his own room, which gave her the idea: wouldn't a
room for two cost the same, or almost the same, as a room
for one? And she deceived him about the food, told him it was
an open buffet for the participants and their guests. That was
a lie; she paid separately for him.

· I have the feeling you're never going to go with me to
that island.

· In this life one never knows.

· Tell me about it, Luci; I'll close my eyes and pretend
I'm traveling. Begin again.

· You have to leave Rio in the afternoon, and after two
hours on the highway you get to the little port, like something
out of an adventure story. There are old sailors with scars,
some of them missing an arm or a leg. And there are barefoot
boys with parrots perched on their shoulders, but everything
is peaceful. Night comes early in the tropics and there are
very few lights there, a few little family-run hotels, immac-
ulately clean, and a block away, hidden behind the trees, some
kind of tavern where they've got everything, even women
who do a striptease if somebody pays, they told us, with ugly
rock music—that was what you'd hear at night in the distance,
not pretty samba music. The village is mysterious because you
get there at night, or almost, and you don't get to see much,
maybe a kerosene lamp in those creepy little shops. And in
the morning the boat leaves so early that there's no time to
see anything. The time we got there in her car night was
beginning to fall, but when she went with the man all the
people in the conference left in two big buses early in the
morning from Rio. Some with companions, who were from all
over the world. There were over forty participants, not counting the others. Up until the last minute he'd said no, that he
had things to do and bills to pay, but she stumped him with
the powerful argument that if he took off a few days to rest
he'd be able to go back to his work with renewed energy. It
was crazy for him to reject a free vacation. The version she
gave him was that each participant could bring a guest and it
was all included in the price of the event, as she put it. Because
it was an independent conference.

· You already told me that.

· Financed by the psychologists themselves.

· They can afford it, with what they charge.

· So, six o'clock that morning, it was still dark when the buses were about to leave. She didn't want to pressure him too much, and so she didn't tell him it was better to sleep over at her house to avoid any problem of delays: the alarm clock might not go off, whatever. But she paid dearly for her discretion, because she was the one who didn't sleep a wink all night long, afraid that he wouldn't wake up in time. She took a taxi to the point of departure, at the Marina Palace Hotel. And there he was, half hidden behind the participants and chatting with the hotel doorman, because he was too shy to talk to anybody else. She couldn't believe her eyes: there he was, he'd surrendered himself to her for at least the seven days of the conference. This Silvia brought with her a medium-sized suitcase, and he brought two, one filled with papers to get some accounting work done. There she began to introduce him to the others; most of them spoke Spanish, and there she got the shock of her life because he spoke our language perfectly, and he'd never said a word to her that wasn't in Portuguese. That's what happens with people here, they have a great facility for languages. She was speechless, she couldn't believe he'd never studied Spanish, and she made him swear to it. Well, there were delays because some inconsiderate people arrived late and the two buses barely got to that port in time to take the daily boat, the only one. After about an hour on the calm sea they began to catch a glimpse of the island.

· Without anybody getting sick?

· Nobody. When I got on the boat at that dock I couldn't open my eyes it was so bright out, even with dark glasses and all, but out at sea I could take the glasses off. The light didn't hurt my eyes anymore; it was clean light without that yellow that's such an irritation.

· Yellow doesn't irritate my eyes, what are you saying?

· I don't like yellow. Old people can be nice-looking if they stay a rosy pink or white, but if they turn yellow they look like they're about to die. And when black people get old they never seem as pitiful as we do. Unless the whites of their eyes turn yellow, because that's when that race has had it too.

· Tell me about the trip those two had, then if you want to you can tell me about yours.

· If you're on the prow you begin to see more and more palm trees, a very light green but never quite yellow, while the water is green too, but on the blue side. And the sand is sometimes white and other times really golden. You see a pure blue sky without the gray of any cloud, nor any amber glare, because that would border on yellow, right? And the two hotels are whitewashed, and when they got there everybody ran to their rooms to close the shutters and rest because they'd all gotten up that morning around four-thirty, or five at the latest. But he didn't let her go to sleep immediately, you know what I mean? And when he was finally finished with her it was almost lunchtime and she had to appear in the dining room without any rest at all, not one minute. Luckily, it was all very informal; they'd put a waiter in a covered patio and he was in charge of the hot and cold buffet; they each went up and served themselves whatever they wanted, and there were several large tables reserved, and everyone sat where they wanted. Not when I went with her, what a difference! You had to sit and wait a long time for the food because there was no buffet, which is the invention of the century. The rest of that arrival day was free, and he was anxious for lunch to be over so he could go see the shrimp boats that were tied up nearby, where there wasn't a soul around because the fishermen sleep till four in the afternoon. At that point she couldn't take it anymore she was so tired, and so she said she didn't want to go along. He'd noticed those boats as soon as they docked, and he went off, happy as could be, to see if any of the owners had appeared yet. It was first time she'd seen him like that, transformed.

· Transformed how?

· Full of enthusiasm, and letting go a little. Until then he'd been holding on to her skirts like a shy little boy hiding from the grown-ups.

· She let him go alone? I can't believe that of her.

· What? She was delighted to go take a siesta; she didn't even want coffee after her lunch, so that she wouldn't stay awake. What she'd really feared was that he'd get bored while she attended the conference. This Silvia noticed that his heart leaped as he got off at the dock and discovered those boats, but it wasn't till lunch that he brought up the subject. They were in line with a few others serving themselves from the buffet when he asked to sit alone with her; he wanted to tell her something. They chose a table way in the back, and there she found out that as a young boy he'd been crazy about sailboats. It's a very common thing here in Rio, but only among people who have money. And it seems his family had had a good income—they gave him everything he wanted as a kid, a membership in a sailing club, for example. This was around thirty years ago, when this country was so rich. And he told her more, about the time he left home because he wanted a life out in the open, because he had the fever for adventure that young men get. He took off and disappeared, went to work at something he really liked, on a fishing boat. But not as a mere peon, no. The boat belonged to the father of a boy who always went sailing with him, all wealthy people. And he worked as a manager of sorts, supervising each day's catch, but he liked the heaviest work best and would get in there with the fishermen to cast the nets and pull them in filled with shrimp. They'd go out in the boat in the late afternoon and be on the open sea all night. A little before dawn they'd begin gathering the nets and at eight in the morning they'd be on their way back to land, where they'd weigh the load and finally go to sleep after a very long workday. The boat didn't set sail from Rio, but from a bay pretty far away. And he'd spent months there without returning. Until his girlfriend went to look for him one day.

· If he already had a girlfriend he couldn't have been so young. But had he wanted to escape from the parents or from the girlfriend?

· From both, I think. But I don't know all the details about his disappearance. This Silvia always says the same thing, that he'd gotten involved with the girl too soon, and his parents didn't like that.

· They didn't like the girl?

· No, the fact that he'd become engaged so young, before graduating. And this Silvia says that when all this friction with the family arose, he took advantage of the commotion and went and broke off with the girlfriend too. If he'd loved her so much he wouldn't have gone off to be a fisherman, don't you think? But she appeared there in front of him one fine day, she'd been searching for him. And they decided to marry, so he came back here to Rio and began to do accounting for individual clients; he never finished his studies in economics and never went back to fishing. Poor boy, eh?

· Really. He's always meeting up with some woman who makes him do what she wants.

· But on the island he was happy again. Those boats still didn't have any caretaker around when he came by after lunch, and he couldn't hold himself back and he got into one, then another, to inspect all the details. He hadn't gotten into one of those things in, I think, over twenty years, back when he'd left all that behind. Something strange came over him when he smelled brine again, and boat food. It's just that when he worked as a young man, around midnight they'd suddenly get terribly hungry on the high seas . . .

· Don't exaggerate; that can't be the high seas, they always stayed near the coast.

· Open sea, then. I was just trying to give you an idea. Well, a few hours after leaving the dock they'd suddenly get hungry as could be, and one of them would grill shrimp on coals, and open cans of ice-cold beer, or if it was cold out they'd gulp down cups of steaming black coffee. And that smell impregnated the wood of the boat, the smell of the freshly ground coffee they toasted right there, and of the juicy pulp of the shrimp as it was getting crunchy.

· Tomorrow fix me some grilled shrimp, be good to me.

· They're very expensive.

· I'll buy them. Go on.

· Luckily, the heavy vapor of the beer gets swept away by the wind, I imagine. And suddenly all those memories came back to him; it was like stepping into the fishing boat of his early youth. Time hadn't passed and there he was, still brim-

ming with health, he'd grown a slight belly but he had his
health. Youth had gone but not his health, so what did a few
gray hairs and lines on his forehead matter?

· And she could get to sleep?

· Of course! As soon as her head hit the pillow. He was
the one who woke her up around six, all excited. He'd been
talking to some of the boatmen and they'd invited him to go
out to sea. Or along the coast, don't look at me that way, I'm
not exaggerating anything.

· To come back the next morning? I don't believe it! He
was leaving her alone the first night?

· She was happy as could be, but he was the one who
wasn't too sure, I think out of fear of offending her, but she
insisted that he go. All she wanted was to have a cup of tea
with him first, something like that, because there were things
she wanted to ask him, if he wanted to go on excursions to
other islands with some other people there, not the participants but their companions. She hadn't dared to bring it up
before. But what was the problem? That if he stopped to have
that tea he'd miss the fishing boats, so she was happy to hurry
him off to the dock, but told him to take some warm clothing.

· She wanted to conquer him no matter what it took.

· You don't get it; she's not overbearing, she's very un-
derstanding. Besides, she loves her work, and during that
first lunch he hadn't let her talk to anybody, so now she'd be
free to make connections with the group at night.

· And that morning when they arrived she'd already gotten what she was after.

· What was that?

· What interested her most was what went on in bed, and
once she got that she didn't care if he went off. But no, you're
right; another woman in her place would have wanted to keep
a tight rein on him.

· Of course! Well, at any rate he went flying off, one of
the boats had already set sail but the other one was still there.
He didn't listen to her and went off without a sweater, since
there wasn't any time to bother looking for it in his suitcase.
It was already getting dark, and once out of the bay the captain

took out some cans of beer in honor of their guest, and he was already anxious for the hours to pass and get to the moment when he could devour a big plate of grilled shrimp.

· Poor thing, that's why he's chubby. He has a big appetite, like me.

· But before stuffing his gullet he was going to get his fill of the main thing, the pure sea air! His lungs filled with that air. In the boat he was all lungs; he had no need for his head because he didn't have to think about figures and calculations for those damn taxes. Pure lung and nothing else, that powerful sea wind filled him with drive, like those sails that fill up and unfold all the way and move ahead smoothly with the wind. He wouldn't have cared if a hurricane were raging around him.

· That's the way most men are, or not?

· What do you mean?

· What they want is to be free and without ties. I hope Ignacio is that way too.

· Yes, I think most of them are that way.

· I don't think Ignacio is going to get involved with the first woman who crosses his path.

· If he likes his freedom he won't. This man told her how much he liked to feel the wind in his face. To himself he probably had the nerve to compare himself to the wind, I'll bet.

· I don't think so; I imagine him as being rather unassuming.

· That's exactly why, it's his other side. Free as the wind and completely irresponsible, demolishing everything in his path and he doesn't look back to see the ravages.

· We're not like that, are we, Luci?

· Like what?

· We don't like the wind. Us women. It ruffles our hair, or brings dust into the house, and makes the windows start banging.

· Now it's fashionable to say that women are really born that way too, wild like them, but that our upbringing changed us. To know beyond the shadow of a doubt if this is true, however, one would have to be born again, don't you think?

· With all this, you said you knew some very naughty things that would shock me. I'm waiting and there hasn't been anything naughty so far.

· You'll see. That night she was very content with the people at the conference; she was able to concentrate on the whole thing and everyone at the meeting stayed up late, a really harmonious group. All of them on the same wavelength.

· But of course: if they were all practically communists they had nothing to fight about.

· I don't agree, some can be more fanatical than others. Anyway, she went to sleep late and got up at seven in the morning when the sun came in, because she still hadn't figured out how to close the shutters properly. And he still hadn't come back. Right there she jumped out of bed without losing a second, because if he gave her the time she could fix herself up a little, first of all brush her teeth, and throw enough water on her face so her eyelids wouldn't look swollen; after forty they're always a telltale sign.

· By your tone of voice I can already tell what's coming. Let's see if I can guess: she had all the time in the world to put on her makeup and he still didn't come.

· You guessed it. She was starting to feel weak in the stomach because she'd already been up for an hour without breakfast. Then she asked them to bring something to her room, but they told her they didn't have room service. And then she got the terrible idea that something might have happened on the high seas. After all, those little boats are pretty rudimentary.

· She's the one who used that expression "high seas," right?

· Yes, Nidia.

· It's obvious that nobody at your house ever went fishing. That's never said; only the big cruisers, the transatlantic ships, travel on the high seas. Learn that once and for all.

· You've already told me a thousand times. Well, that's the way she is, she has a vivid imagination and gets wound up immediately and worries without any reason. So she went to the dining room for breakfast, and already some of the group were there. It was after eight, and the sessions began at nine.

And luckily, talking with her colleagues distracted her a little. Oh, I forgot, she found a woman that morning having breakfast by herself, a Portuguese psychologist who was traveling alone. That day they also had lunch together because the two of them were alone. And so she had some distraction during that tense stretch of time, and the coffee must have revived her a little too.

· Especially the coffee.

· It must have been around a quarter to nine when some-one patted her on the back and it was him, quite dirty and with a growth of beard. He didn't want to have breakfast, because fishermen don't have coffee in the morning; they go to sleep at that hour and get up around three or four in the afternoon. Everybody stared at him because he looked pretty strange compared with the others, who were freshly bathed and shaven. She began to explain it all to everyone at the table, but he cut her short and asked her to go to the room with him for a moment. It's just that he was dead-tired and happy as could be, and wanted to apologize for not coming back earlier. And he asked her to please wake him at noon so they could have lunch together, because he wanted to discuss something with her. And because of the way he was going around in circles, like someone who wants to excuse himself for something, she guessed what was coming, and it was what you can already imagine.

· I don't know.

· Something pretty selfish. Guess.

· I give up.

· He wanted to go out with the fishermen again that night.

· That afternoon you mean, which is even worse. Without having dinner together or anything.

· Exactly. She told him not to worry, that he should sleep until four, which is when she'd have an hour off. And he said no, that she should wake him at noon. But she realized he was saying that to be polite. And she gave him a kiss and went off to the first session of the morning. She couldn't concentrate on a thing; she was very agitated, her mind was working at terrific speed but going round and round in a vicious circle, trying to understand what was happening. On the one hand she was glad that he had something to do, that he wasn't bored, but on the other hand she felt as if events were passing her by. Basically what she didn't like, I think, is that she was finding out he was a stranger to her, and that she was betting too much on something that could turn out to be an utter loss.

· The only time in my life I went to the racetrack I bet on a horse because I liked its name. And it lost, of course. I didn't know if it was a fast runner or not.

· How I wish you'd remember its name.

· Of course I remember, it was Don Clemente, like my father-in-law, who was the nicest man in the world.

· Papa was good too, Nidia. A pity he died so young. Did you ever think how different everything would have been if he hadn't died so young?

· And your husband too; he didn't die young but it was even worse for him, poor Alberto. What happened to him . . .

· One shouldn't think of those things, Nidia. You came to Rio to forget all the sad things. So don't make me remember. Back to the neighbor: this was a letdown for her, up until that point everything had been going so well, but the man was slipping away from her again, like water between her fingers. As the session continued her spirits sank deeper and deeper; all her calculations had really come out wrong, because she was missing out on a very interesting work opportunity, she couldn't concentrate at all, and she wasn't able to solidify anything with him. Suddenly she got terribly depressed, and when the session was over at noon she went to her room to get some papers for the three o'clock session, where she would have to participate. But she entered on tiptoes so as not to wake him. She was determined not to try to force destiny any further. She'd dreamed so much about those days on the island, or rather, about those nights: the moonlight walks with him on the deserted beach and the endless conversations, there on those long nights on the island, without electricity, with time to ask him about everything. Here she confessed to me one thing, that she suffers from what's called professional deformity. That is, she knows everything about her patients, their deepest darkest secrets, and with him she wanted the same thing to happen. She was thirsty to know all, even his earliest

memory. Everything about the past and everything about the
present. So that she'd be able to give him a perfect future,
with every conceivable need well attended to. But she didn't
know what these needs were, or even worse, that what he
needed most was to hop into a fishing boat and never return.
And if she too got into the boat? She'd be a bother in that
world of men, wouldn't she? Besides, she had her life, her
work in Rio. Was it so impossible to find a reasonable man to
get together with at the end of a workday and share a few
hours like civilized people? She entered the room and in total
silence took out the papers. But, who knows why, he woke
up, just as if he'd smelled her. And that's possible, because
she always uses the same French perfume; as soon as the
patients leave she takes her bath and puts on her perfume.
We're alike in that way; once I take my bath and change in
the evening I don't feel dressed unless I put on a drop of
cologne. She immediately apologized for having awakened him
unintentionally, and he on the contrary scolded her for not
having called him. His face was heavy with sleep, and he got
up.
    · Was he dressed?
    · She didn't say.
    · After coming back from fishing all night he must have
taken a bath.
    · Then he probably had no clothes on, Nidia.
    · She didn't mention any details?
    · I don't remember.
    · He hadn't shaved yet, had he?
    · She didn't tell me, because that was such an important
moment for other things that she evidently forgot the details.
You see, he asked her to come sit down next to him on the
bed.
    · Then he must have been covered up with the sheet.
    · Most probably. She sat down and he asked her to give
him her hand, no, both hands, and he grabbed them, both her
hands, and he said that never in his life could he thank her
enough for what she had done for him. Because he had truly
believed that he'd never again feel such happiness in his life.
He'd been convinced, until that day before, that he'd never

again feel a need to thank God for being alive, as he'd felt that dawn on the high seas—sorry, out at sea—when he saw the first rays of sunlight.

· So the sea, or fishing rather, had given him that joy. Not her.

· But she didn't interpret it that way, no, she felt inundated by such great emotion that she gave him a kiss on the forehead and ran out to the patio. She couldn't hold back the need to cry and looked for a corner of the garden where she wouldn't be seen. She felt so satisfied to have made him so happy that she burst into tears and began to shake all over.

· Were they tears of joy?

· Of course.

· I don't think so, Luci. She must have interpreted it that way, but that wasn't why she was crying.

· So you know better than she does?

· She was crying because anything he might say to her affected her, but basically what had happened was bad. She cried because she realized that she wasn't the most important thing to him, period. Why twist things around? When it comes to love affairs, a man either likes you or he doesn't, you win him over or you don't. Why or how that happens . . . who knows, but the results are crystal-clear: if you don't call someone up it's because you don't want to see them, that's all there is to it.

· Hold your horses. She waited till she'd stopped crying, and then had to return to the room because she'd forgotten her papers and it was almost lunchtime. She entered the room again on tiptoes but he was awake, sprucing himself up in the bathroom.

· Shaving.

· Probably. And then came a romantic interlude from his end, I don't know if you get what I mean.

· No.

· Well, he started kissing her all over her body, do you see? But she broke loose because she had to be at lunch already, where they were going to put together the first afternoon session, from three to four-thirty, the one she had to participate in. Then he asked her if she'd be free at four-thirty, because the boat left at five-thirty. Yes, she'd be free, the other session was from six to seven-thirty. Then they said goodbye till later and he begged her to wake him if he was asleep, because he was going to skip lunch, what he wanted was to keep sleeping.

· He'd gone to bed at nine, plus eight hours of sleep, so that's five o'clock, and he was afraid of missing the boat at five-thirty.

· And also he must have had the desire to be with her.

· Less one thing than the other.

· I'll continue. At lunch she was much better now and could concentrate on the discussion, and then the session began very well. There were three presentations twenty minutes each, followed by a half hour of discussion. She spoke and everybody was very interested in what she said. But the third one to speak, a Venezuelan, was already going on thirty-five minutes instead of twenty when the chairwoman of the panel interrupted him. That's where this Silvia started trembling, because the whole program wasn't going to fit in the scheduled hour and a half. The Venezuelan insisted that he had to complete his presentation, just five minutes more, which turned out to be fifteen. And then it was almost four-thirty. The poor thing was such a bundle of nerves that she felt like killing the Venezuelan, who, besides, hadn't said anything new and had spent the whole time attacking a Spaniard who'd spoken that morning. Anyway, things were going badly because they'd still have to hold the discussion after the lectures. And she didn't dare say that she had no time because her boyfriend was waiting for her in the room. But fate intervened: at four-thirty sharp the fellow managing the food services came in and said he had to prepare the tables for the afternoon coffee, as they call it, which we would call the afternoon tea. There was a brief argument, but everything was left for that night after dinner, for those who wanted to come, and she ran to the room. But as she passed in front of the little bar near the reception desk she caught sight of him. He was having something, I forget what, but it wouldn't be coffee, because they don't serve it at that little bar. Or what with the conference, might everything be changed? When I was there they didn't

serve coffee; at any rate, he was cleanly shaven, with fresh
clothes on. And they went immediately to the room. Details
about that she didn't give me. And a little after five he left so
as not to miss the boat. She accompanied him to the dock. And
that second session, according to her, was excellent; nobody
took more time than planned, because they made an an-
nouncement asking them to respect everybody's turn. And at
night she had dinner with the Portuguese woman, who turned
out to be an excellent companion.

· And where's all the spicy stuff you announced? Up until
now there's been barely a tidbit.

· You'll see. Well, that day was really beautiful for her,
because after so many ups and downs everything was straight-
ened out; he'd been very affectionate and besides, I already
told you, reconciled with life. And her presentation had gone
well that afternoon, and on top of it all that Portuguese woman
turned out to be such pleasant company that from that day on
the two of them always had lunch and dinner together.

· Were they the only two single women?

· I think they were—at least, the only two who were
unaccompanied at night. And there were some single men
among the participants, but at night all they did was drink
and drink. And according to her, they were men with inhi-
bitions, because only after getting quite drunk would they
start flirting with the two women; imagine how disgusting for
them. Men are utterly disgusting when they're drunk.

· How old was the Portuguese woman?

· If she hasn't died she must be more or less the same age
as the one next door, she didn't tell me specifically. But the
Portuguese woman wasn't divorced like her, she was a spin-
ster. She'd had some affairs but never any luck, and no children. So life had been better to the one next door, who at
least has her son. Or used to have him, past tense. So the
important thing is that everything worked out very well; they
arrived on a Tuesday, and that same afternoon and Wednesday, Thursday, and Friday he went out with the boatmen, not
Saturday, because it was the only night of the week when they
didn't fish. And everything was perfect because Saturday they
ended the sessions at four-thirty and didn't have that other

one from six or so to eight; that way he could have his siesta
without any problem, and she left him in peace until it was
almost night. At that point she woke him up so that they could
have dinner together in the hotel, and it was only then that
he met the Portuguese woman, and the Portuguese woman
wanted to leave them alone, but they insisted that she join
them. He was very quiet; the one who spoke the most was
the Portuguese woman, who's fanatical about her work and
told them so many things about the psychologists in Portugal.
But the time for the famous walk along the beaches in the
moonlight was drawing near and this Silvia started to get
tense. Because she'd forgotten to tell the Portuguese woman
about all the hopes she had for that walk. She'd dreamed so
much about that walk each night, and up till then nothing, so
she had to take advantage of that Saturday, you see, he was
probably going to go out every night with the fishermen, and
the next Friday everybody at the conference was returning
home. But the Portuguese woman knew what was what, and
when the walk was mentioned she said that she'd let them go
alone. She must have wanted to go with the two of them, but
she realized the situation. And the little couple went off alone,
to walk around the island, and that's what I did with her, with
a full moon, and it's beautiful; you can go around the whole
island in a little over an hour. And that was really the only
time they were alone with time to talk, and he asked her all
about the sessions and told almost nothing about himself. A
little bit about when he'd left his parents' home, but when he
came to why he left his fiancée and why they got back together,
there he stopped. She saw that he was happy, as if in another
world, and that's why she didn't try to bring up the subjects
that most interested her, that is, everything about his daily
life in Rio, down to the very last detail. Although around then
what she most wanted to know was why he'd left his fiancée,
in that interval of freedom he had in his life. And since you
asked about spicy details, she told me a rather shameful intimate thought: she imagined that at some moment he would
take her clothes off to see her in the moonlight; she was dying
to see if she would look better, fresher, younger, with her
skin illuminated by that famous silver light of the moon. But

he didn't try anything, and besides, she hadn't figured on one
thing: at night you can get a pretty cool breeze, and it makes
you feel like going to sleep and covering up nice and warm,
after washing the sand off your feet. And when they got back
to the hotel he invited her to have a drink of something strong,
because they'd gotten a little chilled. She and I also had a good
shot of cognac after that walk. I hadn't wanted to take the
walk, not for fear of tiring myself out but for her, so as not
to stir things up. But that was what she wanted, to stir them
up, and she succeeded. And that was the worst moment of
our stay there, because it was really hard for her to believe
what had happened afterward. "How can someone give up
happiness?" she said to me. "Because he was happy during
those days! Of that I'm sure!"

  · Don't mix things up, first tell all about their trip, then
about yours.

  · About that night I don't know anything further. They
had that drink; she was worried—when wasn't she?—that he
wouldn't be able to sleep, because he'd inverted his normal
sleep schedule for several days in a row already, but he wanted
them to go to bed just the same, around midnight, and he
managed to sleep very well.

  · And her?

  · I think she did too. It was the only night they slept
together. And now finally comes the naughty part.

  · He didn't want to get up for breakfast.

  · You guessed it. When he woke up he was all enthusiastic,
incredibly happy. It's that he hadn't seen anything of the island
yet! The plan was to go to the beach, take a little basket they
prepared for them at the hotel—a picnic in the jungle—because on Sunday there's no food service at midday. When we
were there too they gave us the little Sunday basket.

  · Good food?

  · Yes, two kinds of delicious salads, slices of apple with
diced nuts, a very juicy apple, that was one, and another with
grated carrots and orange slices, a combination they do here.
I never imagined that carrots would combine so well with
oranges.

  · I've seen it advertised at juice bars. It sounded disgusting to me. But just see, the next time I'm going to try it.

· There are very few tropical flavors that I like. Mangos and cherimoyas make me a little nauseous.

· You never liked to try exotic things. You distrust them from the start.

· That's not true; I'd never tried the maracujá and now I'd do anything for that juice, if you add sugar to it. Well, besides the salads they give you slices of roasted chicken, and bread and dessert.

· But did they get up in time for breakfast or not?

· He didn't want to. He felt like lying around, but her stomach was so empty that she felt dizzy and had to tell him frankly that she couldn't live on love alone.

· Had he awakened her during the night?

· Oh, Nidia, she didn't give me those details. She told me that he gave the impression of liking her a lot in that way, because every afternoon, at the only moment they were in the room together, well, the inevitable always happened. But she didn't say a thing about that night; they slept very well, that she did say, and he didn't want to get up.

· But, Luci, you'll have to forgive me but you said that there were naughty things. And there's not a damn thing naughty about what you're telling me.

· You be quiet. As I was saying, she was dying for a drop of coffee and the two finally got to the dining room to have breakfast. And that's where they give you the little baskets.

· But why didn't he want to get up?

· From what happened later, during the picnic, I imagine it was because they'd done it that morning, before breakfast. But she didn't give me any details. Then there in the breakfast room was the Portuguese woman, and the woman next door felt obliged to invite her to go with the two of them. Because the truth is that every day the woman had been wonderful company, and it's not nice at mealtime to look for a place to sit only to end up alone or else at a table where you're not wanted. So the three of them went out. It was a beautiful day; the sun was strong just every once in a while, which helped a lot because one can't stand too much sun. And they walked along beaches, all of them deserted, because almost all the

others in the group had gone out boating. And of course they
didn't, because he'd done enough boating all those nights. And
the Portuguese woman was prone to seasickness. Then they
went along that string of little beaches; I saw them all, the
first one that was all white, then another one with craggy
rocks, good for looking at the bottom with those special
glasses. I didn't like the idea of it and didn't want to try it,
until this Silvia got a little angry and told me I'd be silly to
miss such a sight. She got quite serious, almost scolded me.
And I'm grateful to her for it, you see, I didn't want to cause
any useless tension and so I forced myself and overcame the
fear of looking under the water. It was divine! That bottom
with colored rocks, and the reflections from the sun following
the movement of the waves. It was something out of this
world. And then comes the jungle itself, where there's nice
shade to sit in and eat when you get hungry. Well, the three
of them had a nice swim; he went out pretty far and she got
a little scared. Because she's on the anxious side, that's a defect
of hers. And back from swimming they ate a bit, she barely
ate half her basket or less, but he finished off his and hers too.
And even though he hadn't had anything to drink, after eating
he seemed changed, because he talked and talked. Now, something had happened in the water while they were together on
top of a rock, wondering whether to dive or not, because those
rocks were high, I saw those rocks, something like nine or
twelve feet more than . . .

· They went into the water right after eating?

· No, before eating, when he climbed up on those rocks
he began to show signs of that euphoria that came over him.
He was there getting ready to dive and the Portuguese woman
shouted to him from far off that he should jump in, that she
wanted to see a fancy flip. And he burst out laughing. The
woman next door didn't know why he was laughing so much,
and he didn't want to say. And finally he told her that he felt
like a movie star showing off for his female admirers. And she
said that she did declare herself an admirer of his, but not to
count on the Portuguese woman, because she was a rather
distant sort. This made him laugh more than ever.

· Why?

· That's what this Silvia asked him. And he laughed and
laughed. She was delighted to see him so happy, but also
intrigued by that mysterious laughter. And he told her the
Portuguese woman was stealing looks at him where she
shouldn't from time to time when he wasn't looking—out of
the corner of his eye he could see her doing it. You realize
what I'm telling you, right? The Portuguese woman was looking at his fly.

· But men's bathing trunks don't have a fly.

· But what that poor woman liked to watch . . . was what
was underneath the fly, is that clear?

· She couldn't keep her eyes off him, poor thing. But why
did that make him laugh?

· Because suddenly he was there like some great movie
star, and when he found himself the center of everyone's attention he began walking without his usual slouch, and trying
to hold in his belly.

· How did he look in bathing trunks?

· I never saw him, Nidia, with or without bathing trunks.
And after eating he told them about those nights of fishing,
of how you always have to keep your eye on the sea, because
a storm could burst at any moment, but an experienced sailor
can feel the storm coming. Those boats are pretty rickety and
can't stand up to a rough storm, they have to get closer to the
coast as soon as the wind begins to change. He said that was
what he liked the most, to be there listening to the breathing
of the sea, to have his ear against its very heart. And to guess
its changes. Sometimes all at once the sea begins to swell, its
heart starts beating fast, without any apparent reason. And
he added that the sea is sometimes like the body of a woman,
that one has to know how to listen to its rhythm, so as to
dominate it in some way, or no, that's not what he said, to
know how to anticipate what she wants. And as he talked the
Portuguese woman looked at him very impressed, and this
one next door began to observe her, to see if she was looking
where she shouldn't. And once she caught her in the act. And
then this Silvia had a strange impulse. She asked them to
excuse her because she wanted to be alone for a while, she
wanted to walk and to think by herself, and the other two

were a bit taken aback, and this Silvia winked at him and went off for a walk.

· I don't believe you.

· She didn't believe herself. She says that she felt such great pity for the other woman, and that it seemed unfair for one to have so much and the other nothing, that she felt an impulse to lend him to her for a while.

· But the other two must have been surprised.

· Think, Nidia, all this was happening in a setting very different from the everyday, that green goes to your head like alcohol. And this Silvia began to wander around, she climbed up to the diving rock again, but from there she couldn't see anything that might be happening. One question I want to ask you, did you ever see a drowned person getting mouth-to-mouth respiration?

· No, luckily, never.

· It's very upsetting. Here living by the beach one sees it from time to time. Those big lifeguards in red undershirts who rush into the water when they see somebody sinking, and once they're on the sand, if the drowned man doesn't react they bend him over several times, and if he still doesn't breathe they open his mouth and blow hard inside. And of course it's even more striking when it's a drowned woman, because this great big kid gets on top of her and it's all very overwhelming, that big animal bringing the dead woman back to life. And then the woman next door came down off the rock and went over to the next beach, I don't remember what it's like, and then she came walking back slowly, to give them time for something. But she decided to return without making any sound with her steps; the irresistible temptation to spy came over her. Would he be bringing that poor woman, so neglected by the world, back to life?

· But the Portuguese woman wasn't so down and out.

· According to her, at one point the Portuguese woman had a terrible expression on her face, a look of total desolation, when he spoke about the storms at sea.

· But he didn't do it on purpose; he's a good man.

· This Silvia felt that she almost had the right to spy,

because they couldn't push her aside; after all, hadn't it been her idea to leave them alone? And then something happened that made her rather nervous: she got lost and couldn't find the way back to them. But she didn't want to call to them either, because that would put them on their guard. She decided not to lose her calm, to take a deep breath, not let her nerves choke her up, and keep looking. But nothing, and still nothing. At last she suddenly heard something, like a woman panting as if she were drowning, and struggling to escape death, because death wants to drag you down to the bottom of the water; even the clear water of that rocky beach could kill you all the same. And the woman next door looked and it was them, without any clothes, him on top almost covering her all up, and kissing just as he'd kissed *her* in the hotel room hours before, while trying to pass the oxygen into her, which he had a surplus of but which she lacked. He was mounted on top of her, but he wasn't wearing the little black bathing trunks and red undershirt of the lifeguards, he didn't have anything on. It was a strange thing: this man she loved so much was also an animal that didn't deserve the slightest trust. She looked for a second and then stepped back so that they wouldn't realize she was watching them. And she walked farther away without making any noise, and a good while later she pretended to be lost and called to them, to give them time to put themselves together. And when she saw them she hugged them and told them she'd had such a nice walk, and that she was exhausted, and the three of them lay resting there for a while. Like a fool, the woman next door couldn't relax and sleep as the other two could, and after a bit she woke them and asked them to go for a swim with her. They accompanied her and the three of them swam together, and afterward they returned because his boat would be leaving before six. According to this Silvia, from the moment she saw him on top of the other woman she knew that he was the only one who could pass her that oxygen she herself lacked, because day by day she was drowning, without him little by little her lungs were filling with dirty water. And that night at dinner the Portuguese woman told her that she'd never known any-

body more generous than her, and this one smiled at her eva-
sively and asked her not to speak any further about the matter,
but she did ask her to tell her everything about her life.

· She treats everybody like patients.

· Look, that's nonsense. With me it's exactly the opposite,
I never told her anything about me, because there's barely
enough time for her to tell me about herself; besides, she
repeats each thing at least ten times. Well, the rest of the
days on the island were the same routine. He'd go out in the
late afternoon with the boatmen and come back in the morning
when she was about to go to her group meetings, and they
saw each other only when she returned from the first session
in the afternoon. There he was, already waiting for her, cleanly
shaven and smiling from ear to ear, because the great adventure of casting those empty nets was drawing near, every
night the same thing, although deep down there was always
that fear that the storm would burst, without time to reach
the shelter of the bay. He didn't see the Portuguese woman
anymore, only from a distance.

· And where did he eat? Was the shrimp at night enough?

· Oh, I forgot something; this is important. From the second day that he began going out to sea she realized that he
was missing lunch, because at midday he felt more like sleeping. Then she spoke with the dining room manager and every
night they made him up a little basket, which they left in the
refrigerator, and he'd eat it when he came back in the morning.

· And to drink?

· She'd bring him a nice cold beer to the room. And he'd
eat everything in total peace, after having a shower. Then go
to sleep. While she went off to her first session.

· And he thought it all was paid for as part of the group.
Or did he suspect something?

· She paid for everything, to the last cent, without him
suspecting. And Friday morning, when the fishing boat
moored, she was waiting for him at the dock. A little while
later their boat back to shore would be leaving, with the whole
group on board, on their way home. She had prayed for him
to be late so that they'd miss the passenger boat and have to
wait till the next day. But no, he arrived on time, and on the

other dock the buses were right on time waiting, and so now nothing could prevent their separation. On the bus when they caught sight of the first outskirts of Rio he put his lips close to her ear and told her that never in his life would he forget those days, and he owed it all to her.

· And what were his eyes like at that moment? Did he look her in the eye or was he still looking around?

· She didn't mention it. There in the bus one of those uncontrollable impulses came over her and she told him the truth was the other way around, it was she who owed everything to him, and that she now had no control over her actions, that she needed him, his support. That it was too late for her to back out, and in order to continue on . . . without him she couldn't take one more step.

· Poor thing. She really needed him.

· I think that those foolish words of a woman in love did her in. That was her big mistake.

· Why? Why not be sincere?

· Because she never saw him again. That day they said goodbye in front of the Hotel Marina Palace, the final destination of the charter bus. She thought he'd accompany her home in a taxi, as a gesture, a courtesy.

· Now I realize, he was the spoiled one, not her. Poor Silvia, she made a mistake.

· But he was worried about all the work that had piled up; on the island he hadn't even opened the suitcase with all his accounting papers. That felt like a bad sign to her, saying goodbye on the sidewalk, in front of everybody. But the next day, Saturday, they were going to get together. He called her that next morning to tell her he was terribly behind in his work and might call her Sunday at noon, depending on how it went with his papers. He didn't call her. He never called her again.

· Luci, today the telephone rang a lot. But I didn't want to answer.

· Why?

· That impulse came over me. But now I'm sorry.

· Nidia, that was wrong.

· Now I'm sorry.

· Don't do it again.

· Luci, I don't feel anymore like going to the island.

· But it's lovely; what fault is it of the island if people are crazy?

· Luci, I think somebody's at the door. The intercom.

· What time is it?

· It's not light out yet . . . Wait. Three-twenty.

· It must be some drunkard, at this hour.

· You answer, they don't understand me when I speak.

· Wait a minute . . . Nidia, it's the watchman next door. She's in bad shape.

7

To be delivered to Senhora Luci

Luci:

You were here just a while ago and we spoke about the Mexican, the famous Avilés. I had promised to explain to you how his eyes were, his look, but then I didn't manage to communicate anything to you. Maybe I felt ashamed to say certain things. How absurd, I have nothing to lose, I'm defeated, abandoned, humiliated now, to an almost intolerable point. A good thing I said almost. Perhaps in a while it will be intolerable, period. Without the almost. If that happens, I'll call you, Luci. I have no one else to bother. That's the role that's been chosen for you to play, the neighborly wet towel. But it's possible, Luci, that I won't call you tonight; a miracle could happen. You know which. The telephone could ring. My telephone. A telephone that's out of order. I would run to answer, not like your sister Nidia. But I'm not going to ask for a miracle. Something less than that—for example, being able to describe to you Avilés's eyes—could relieve me. And that's why I grabbed pen and paper.

But this doesn't look like my handwriting, Luci; I'm really in bad shape, it's unsteady, as if the letters no longer had that imaginary line upon which I always knew how to place them.

I always wrote straight without needing lines; my handwriting would trace that perfect horizontal line. Instead, this hand-writing today corresponds to a psyche that has suffered a definite and fundamental deviation. It's that I've lost some-thing fundamental. I don't see any point to getting out of bed in the morning and initiating the everyday ritual. Washing my face, picking the newspaper up from the floor . . .

But I'm not being as precise as I'm trying to be; there is indeed something I'd still like to do in this life, and that is to explain to you what the expression in Avilés's eyes meant. I have promised it to you so often. Besides, I want to know its meaning too. Let me concentrate a moment. For example, I'd enter the university library where he was working, and his eyes would have another look because he had some obnoxious book in his hands or was with some exasperating student, and suddenly upon seeing me his eyes would change; without pro-nouncing a word, he was saying that he needed me and that I was exactly the person he had wanted to see appearing through that enormous door in the library. Do you understand?

But I'm not managing to explain to you anything specific, really. That would be the same look of a beggar when you go over to him and give him some money. It was much more than that. That look couldn't be had by someone who was contem-plating a landscape devastated by the wind or whipped by a torrential rain or, even worse, a sky pierced by lightning. A look like his belongs on someone who doesn't remember, or never even knew, what it is to have physical pain, or a bitter memory. The look of a person who has forgotten all the bad things in this world, or who forgets at that moment, because he's looking at someone he loves, or rather, more precisely, at someone who resolves everything in his life.

I don't know, but maybe I was really the one who forgot about those bad things in this world when looking at him. It was my feeling. I didn't make him forget anything, because it's already been proven that things between us didn't end well. How could I know what he felt when he looked at me? So now we're back at zero: the look in his eyes, how was it? I told you that Ferreira's eyes looked, and this is true, like the eyes of a lost little boy, not totally lost, maybe just a bit off the track, and who then sees somebody who knows the way back home, and that makes him happy and tranquil; he recovers peace. Ferreira never called again, Luci. That's also like a little boy, that lack of consideration, that cruelty.

But I'm mixing it all up. Impossible to analyze, to guess what the two of them felt, one just as much as the other, when they looked at me, and made me believe in that fable. Luci, they made me believe that when I appeared all their problems were over. Now I know that they weren't over, or that I created a new series of other, also unsolvable ones. A new series of problems that by not seeing me anymore they solved instantaneously. Or not. Luci, I don't know what my error was; I tried to help them, both of them, by giving them solutions, not headaches. I didn't ask for much. Only that they see me. In my free hours, which weren't many. Good hours to meet, at night, for busy people like us. Ideal.

Where did I go wrong? Luci, I think you're going to agree with me, yes, I see it so clearly at this precise moment. I let them see my desperation. I let them see that by the age of forty-six I had only succeeded in increasing the vulnerability I always had. I've worked so much, studied so much, made such an effort for things to go well. I've traveled, I've tried to adapt myself to different countries, I've studied and learned to love them as much as my own Argentina. And all I've gotten out of it is this, to depend on a telephone call that will enable me to continue breathing.

I'm alone waiting for someone to ring the doorbell, waiting for my son to write me saying that he no longer likes Mexico and wants to return to Rio, hoping you won't leave the house so you can answer the telephone, and at worst, hoping your sister will answer the telephone and understand a complicated message in Portuguese. Everything that was in my power to resolve I've resolved, but when it's the others' turn then everything is in danger. Everybody else refuses me a tinker's dam, whatever that is. Could it mean that they take me for a tinker's dame, or that they just don't give a damn? Anyway, all jokes aside, perhaps it would be more clarifying to investigate just what I was feeling as I fell under their gaze. About them I know nothing, I never really succeeded in knowing what they felt.

So, Luci, if it doesn't bother you, I'm going to try to explain my side of things once again. When Avilés would look at me, at that moment in which I'd deceive myself thinking that I had restored a spiritual balance in him, I'd feel . . . I'd feel . . . Well, in order to clarify things I'm obliged to play this game of associated images that I sometimes practice with my patients. Both Avilés and Ferreira would make me fantasize about very sturdy roofs that would let through not even a drop of the deluge outside. Avilés lived in an apartment near the university, at the foot of a hill, Ajusco, which attracts awesome electrical storms. I lived in fear of those flashes of lightning, but nobody would pay any attention when I spoke about it, they'd take it as something normal. In Mexico City it rains every afternoon in the summer, and those flashes of lightning strike everywhere you look. One morning I read in the newspaper that lightning had killed someone walking along the very same avenue, with a row of trees down the middle, that I always crossed to go to Avilés's apartment. Trees with white-backed leaves that attract electricity.

He advised me not to be afraid of it, because fear attracts it, like the white or almost silver side of the leaves—what's that tree called? I couldn't resist, and I began to look at the news about accidents in the papers: quite often lightning had killed somebody. But when Avilés looked at me and said lightning didn't kill, I believed it. Though he didn't actually say anything, you see? It was the look in his eyes that spoke. When lightning bolts strike someone who isn't afraid of them, the honey, one might say, that covers the skin of certain people puts them out. Tonight I don't even have any skin, just raw hide, dry, wrinkled, hanging from my bones. Lightning falls menacingly, furiously, but sweet skin puts it out, even sending off some pretty sparks, like fireworks.

If instead of receiving me in his apartment Avilés were to take me tonight to the hills, to one nearby, the terrifying Ajusco, of course, and a terrifying rainstorm broke out, what would happen? Let's suppose that he had insisted upon going this weekend to a hut hidden way up on that hill. I'm simply imagining, understand, Luci? And he would then assure me that there wasn't going to be any problem with the electricity in the air. We'd get to the hut soaking wet, and inside there would be towels, and from the window he shows me how the lightning strikes, and how it kills age-old trees, God knows why, burning them to the ground, and I believe everything he tells me: whoever is not afraid of the storm can go out and receive them; the lightning bolts are our brothers in creation and do nothing to people with skin sweet from so many caresses received that same afternoon. Avilés knew everything about appeasing groundless fears.

How many years it has been since he looked at me in that way. What mistake did I make with him? I told him that I loved him; I criticized his alcoholic excesses; I wanted to make him happier, I wanted to change him. That is, I broke every rule in the book. And with Ferreira? Useless to rack my brains any further. It all ended badly and that's it. But I'm being unfair: I told you all that about the island, I didn't lie about anything, but I left out a fundamental aspect of this sad story. I felt ashamed to tell you about it.

Do you remember that first time he came to see me at the house, that Saturday morning? Everything happened just as I told you, but at a certain moment, while we were still lying in bed, a few seconds after he climaxed, he got sick. He got very nauseous, and it took him a lot of effort not to vomit. I don't think one has to run to a psychology book to understand what happened. A guilt attack as violent as it was primitive. Or rejection toward me. Or whatever it was. The important thing is that it happened. I wasn't good for him, that's all, I was bad for him. I made him sick, like a cheap drink, or fish that was no longer fresh. For me he was a panacea, and I for him a poison. Doesn't this have its comic side? He felt very ashamed, because the urge to vomit had been obvious. I pretended not to notice the psychological aspect, and I offered him some bicarbonate. He took it.

And the next encounter was on the island, without any upsets. Now you know everything. As a little girl when at times I had indigestion, or had a tummyache as one would say, they'd give me something to induce vomiting; it was called ipecac, and on the bottle it read "vomitive substance." That man reduced me to the status of this ipecac, a vomitive substance. He doesn't want to return, because this is the house where he almost threw up on a naked woman with a look of love on her face, or better, the look of an idiot. But, Luci, it so happens that I'm very tired. I can't make the effort to live without his help. He's a man who resolves everything for me. He gives me all the answers. He makes me feel sexy, young. He gives me joy, he makes everything seem interesting to me, everything, as long as he forms part of it all. Seldom in my life have I felt that, the indisputable joy of living, and I'm not resigned to losing it. I refuse to resign myself to the pain. Accepting the pain means accepting death in life. I much prefer death itself. If we don't see each other again, Luci—a big hug.

· Nidia, are you feeling a little better?

· More or less.

· Don't frighten me, please. Tell me clearly what you feel.

· Just sick in general. Like when Emilsen got sick, the exact same thing. Seeing her ill made me ill.

· And did it last a long time?

· Until she got a little better.

· You already heard what they said in the clinic: she's out of danger.

· You should have stayed to keep her company, at least the first twenty-four hours.

· She didn't want me to, how many times do I have to repeat it to you? "Go to your sister," she said to me. But she said it very seriously. What with the tranquilizer, she was going to sleep anyway. And this afternoon they're already sending her home, and that's it.

· Oh, Luci, I can't find a comfortable position in this bed.

· Try to relax, if we could sleep a little now, then later . . .

· I can't sleep during the day!

· . . .

· "You take care of yourself," Emilsen would say to me when I looked worried about her.

· You were here when the doctor spoke to us; after they clean out the stomach there's no longer any danger. So don't get ill because of that.

· What do I care about her? Others want to live and they die. And she, who's lucky to have been cured, goes messing around with pills.

· I think that deep down she didn't want to die. Her liver rejected the pills because she'd had a good dinner. She was still digesting.

· Someone desperate doesn't eat, Luci. But just the same I was upset; I don't like to be entering hospitals again.

· You felt sorrier for her than I did, why is that?

· Was it the emergency ward or an operating room where you saw her?

· I don't know. But now you relax, don't pester me anymore. She's sleeping now, that you can be sure of. So let's us sleep too. And if she comes back in the evening we'll be rested enough to attend to her.

· She's not going to want to see me. But all the same I don't believe they'll let her leave the clinic so soon.

· Her stomach didn't tolerate the pills and that's that; when she threw up everything she was saved. If not she'd already be in the other world.

· If it had been a building like this, without a twenty-four-hour doorman, she'd have died.

· At the condominium meeting I asked them to hire a night watchman; if we each chipped in for a measly little salary we wouldn't even feel it. But they don't want to; they say that as soon as all the cars are parked in the garage the fellow falls asleep and doesn't watch over anything.

· But if someone calls from an apartment asking for help the watchman wakes up.

· She was vomiting everything, even if the watchman hadn't come to the rescue she'd have been saved all the same.

· I'm going to tell you something, but don't tell her. While you were calling the emergency number I took advantage of the moment to look over the house, and I caught the watchman taking something out of the refrigerator.

· Well, I'd asked him for some ice so we could wipe her forehead with cold rags; it was burning up.

· I know that. Afterward he returned to the refrigerator because he must have seen food and was rummaging around when he saw me and dropped everything. Poor boy.

· Poor thing, despite the scare he didn't forget his hunger.

· Luci, it's been a long time since I stayed up all night, and now I'm turning around and around in this bed and I can't find a comfortable position.

· Would you like to eat something?

· No, Luci. What I'd like is something I don't dare tell you.

· You want to go out for a walk.

· Yes, it's nice outside, cloudy, there isn't that strong sun that hurts the eyes.

· Oh, Nidia. I don't even have the energy to go to the bathroom, much less to get dressed and go out. I swear, I've been wanting to go to the bathroom for a while now and I'm so tired I can't even move.

· It's just that the walls are bad for me, Luci, they don't let me breathe.

· Tell me the truth: are you afraid the neighbor's going to have some complication?

· No. She asked for it, I don't feel that sorry for her.

· Then why such a fuss?

· I don't know, Luci. And if that phone call was from him I still don't think it would have made much of a difference. If it was him he was probably calling to make some excuse, not to tell her he was coming over.

· Nidia, now listen to me carefully, because if he calls and you answer you might put your foot in it. She's very lucid now, after the lavage, and the orders are very clear: if he calls, don't tell him anything.

· I got that already.

· Now she hates him, for being inconsiderate. And she's right, because nobody should be treated that way, ignored like a dog.

· Luci, I'm on his side and I'll keep on defending him. She was the one who insisted on the relationship. She was the one who took him out for coffee, she was the one who looked for him afterward and moved heaven and earth until she found him. She was the one who deceived him into going to that hotel, saying it was all free. He wasn't the one to build up her hopes and promise her things.

· You're right, Nidia.

· However it may be, I don't want to answer the phone.

· You might be left alone for a moment if I'm in the shower and my son calls from Switzerland. One should always answer a call.

· When you go into the shower just disconnect the phone.

· In any case, if he calls tell him that she left Rio and went to São Paolo for a few days and that you don't know when she's coming back.

· Luci, if I paid that poor young watchman a few cents, wouldn't he take me out for a little walk?

· I think so.

· You always see some little old man on the beach, or some little old woman, walking with a male nurse or a doorman who lends an arm. I don't need to lean on anybody, but I don't like going out alone.

· Good idea.

· You think the boy must have gone home?

· Oh, Nidia, I never see him in the morning; he must leave very early.

· When I caught him in the refrigerator he looked at me with a face that broke my heart. Those eyes, so beautiful, like a little deer's, always frightened. Not only last night with the open refrigerator. Whenever you look at him he puts on that expression, as if you were catching him red-handed. And each time you brought up the subject of the eyes of the neighbor's men I thought of this boy's eyes.

· I'd never noticed.

· How can you say that? He's such a handsome boy that he immediately draws your attention. I noticed him as soon as I got here.

· It must be that one gets used to it in Rio. The girls on the beaches here, I've never seen bodies like those anywhere. And the boys have adorable faces. Ah! I forgot one thing. This

Silvia was explaining another matter to me as I left her alone in the room, before we came back here. Her despair over his phone call had a special reason, which is that yesterday morning she'd left him a message to call her at this number, that she needed him urgently.

· I don't understand.

· Yes, she'd held back from calling him all this time, since the island.

· But where did she leave the message?

· At one of those offices. Because he never gave her his home phone. That I already explained to you.

· No, Luci, you never made that clear to me.

· Horrible, isn't it? But that's the way it is, he never gave her his home phone, maybe he let it slip, who knows.

· I thought he was so poor that he didn't have a telephone.

· He does, Nidia.

· Then he kept his distance from the very beginning. He's a louse.

· So, since the island she hadn't heard his voice. But when her telephone broke down again two days ago she couldn't take it any longer and called to give him this number, just in case he thought of calling.

· And on top of that she said it was urgent.

· Yes.

· Then that was him who called last night, when I didn't answer. And I did it on purpose.

· How do you know? It could have been a call from Switzerland, and it's just as well you didn't answer, you would have made my son waste a call. Just as well you didn't answer.

· When did Ñato tell you he was coming back?

· He should have been back by now. I don't like the situation one bit.

· I don't think they'll convince him to stay there.

· I didn't say a word to him about not wanting to go live in Lucerne, but he realized it.

· How horrible if he tells you to suddenly pick up and go; Rio will be over for me too.

· No, he has to come back here. Don't scare me. Maybe he was the one who called last night.

· No, I'm sure it was that Ferreira.

· Tell the truth, you answered.

· Yes, Luci, I answered. And it was a Brazilian. But I didn't understand what he said and I hung up. That impulse came over me, I swear I don't know why.

· Nidia . . .

· I got nervous and hung up. He must have given her last name, I don't know. They were strange names.

· Her name is Silvia Bernabeu.

· I did the wrong thing, didn't I?

· If she finds out she'll kill you.

· It was a sudden impulse, Luci, I don't know why I did it.

· I hope she never finds out.

· Luci! The street bell!

· So early? Go see who it is, Nidia, I'm too bushed to get up.

· I don't understand what they say to me through the intercom.

· Go, please. I don't think it's him.

· I don't like it one bit, ringing the bell at this hour . . .

· Luci, it wasn't anything.

· You're crazy; I told you never to open the door to people you don't know.

· I opened it because it was the boy from next door. Look what he brought you.

· My glasses!

· Nothing escapes that boy. You left them on her night table.

· And why did you take so long? Did he tell you something new?

· No, about the neighbor, nothing. He told me that he cleaned up the bathroom, as you asked him to.

· And in all this time that's all he told you?

· No, it's just that I asked him if he wouldn't mind taking me for a little walk for a few blocks. Now. But he couldn't, he had to go sleep at a place where they don't let him in after seven A.M. This evening he's going to explain the whole thing to me. And in principle he accepted the idea of taking a walk. But now he had to hurry off, God knows why.

· Nidia, I can't accompany you now, really.

· It doesn't matter, Luci, I'm feeling better now.

· I heard you open the door to the big closet. If you grabbed some candy you're misbehaving, you can't eat chocolate. If you're hungry there's fruit and you have the maracujá juice I fixed for you. That's what it's for, for you to have it.

· No, it's just that I remembered those meringues from about a week ago were there in the closet and nobody's touched them. I gave one to the boy.

· You did well, Nidia. If he comes this evening tell him to take them all. Pure sugar and beaten egg whites, they couldn't be bad for you but you don't eat them.

· I find them too sweet.

· But they wouldn't do you any harm, and they can fool your sweet tooth.

· Unfortunately, I like everything that's bad for me. Chocolate, wine, liqueurs, fried eggs.

· Ay, Nidia, I just felt a little weak in the stomach.

· Shall I bring you some grapes?

· No, since you're up, bring me a meringue.

8

Dear Nidia:

Here I am writing from the devil's hill. Who would have thought it a week ago. The trip was good, luckily I insisted on traveling economy class; it was empty in the back and a sweet Varig stewardess gave me a row of five seats and I went to sleep as soon as they took the dinner tray away. A nice, relaxed girl with the good manners of the people back there. Here, Nidia, people are so tense that they intimidate me. Why are they so obnoxious if they have everything they need? The women especially. When this Brazilian stewardess returns home, I'm sure she has to do everything, cook, take care of her kids, and just the same she maintains her good humor—and this without a cent in the bank. Look what I got onto talking about instead of telling you about the important things.

Well, things here got cleared up, it was what you said, Ñato wants to accept the transfer to Lucerne. It's a big step ahead in his career, but he didn't feel like deciding without first knowing my opinion. Poor thing, I brought him into the world, so I know him better than he thinks. For me he's transparent. I think the poor thing harbored the hope that when I saw

Lucerne I'd change my mind, when I saw how beautiful and clean and orderly it is.

Nidia, I feel so sad that I can't hide it from you. It's that for him I'm being a bother and, poor thing, he doesn't know how to pretend otherwise. That's what I believe, that he was expecting the miracle that I would like this icebox, this tomb. Yes, Nidia, Lucerne is lovely, but I'm eighty-one, and I have arthritis and every other illness under the sun, you name it, I have it. In that nice heat in Rio, and with such calm, attentive people who serve you so well, I can get along.

But I swear, I don't have the energy to deal with another move to a different country. I don't know how I'm going to do, because I can't stay here. It was one thing to live alone in Rio, with my son a half block away, so that if anything happened to me he could be there with me in five minutes. Here, besides, everything is so expensive that we'd have to live together, I believe. And we won't be able to stand each other. I've acquired a taste for independence, a little late but it's here to stay. Ay, Nidia, how happy I was in Rio and I didn't realize it.

I don't see any other way out, I'm going to have to move here. Anyway, don't you worry, because in a few days I'll return, to close the apartment or whatever's needed. I hope you're not feeling too lonely, but the truth is I'm so grateful to you for staying to take care of my plants instead of returning to Buenos Aires.

I liked how you put your foot down with your son. They're afraid that alone something will happen to us, a sudden breakdown, a charming stroke, and without anybody around to help us. It makes sense for them to think like that. But we shouldn't let them put ideas in our heads, because if not we couldn't even go to the bathroom alone.

That's what's good about the telephone, that one can be more in control. But when you see the worried look they get on their faces, afraid for one's life, that's where you give in, you don't want to see them suffer. If you'd seen the expression on Ñato's face when we spoke about closing the two apartments in Rio, it would have made your heart sink.

I told him that Lucerne seemed lovely to me, but later he caught me crying and he's no fool. Yes, there is the possibility of getting used to it, in time. He says that here there are indoor pools with warm water for my swimming, something very difficult to get there in Rio, but aside from that I'd be stuck in the house all those cold months. About eight a year. And the language . . . Luckily, there's a TV station in Italian.

And friends. I didn't make many in Rio, but something is something. And I don't feel at all easy about the neighbor; if you paid attention to me and wrote me three days after I left, then tomorrow your letter could already arrive. I hope you haven't gotten lazy about writing, the good part is that then you'd have to take the little walk to the post office.

I didn't understand why you wouldn't come to the airport. If it was so that the neighbor could tell me more things, it wasn't necessary; she has more trust in you now and would have said everything in front of you. Not in the car, because the driver was there, but in line waiting to check the baggage there was time to talk without rushing. She was very grateful for all your worrying that morning the man called; it was in the cards that you had to answer the phone! The truth is, that morning I couldn't resist inspecting her apartment, to see if everything was in order, if the watchman had cleaned up that mess in the bathroom. Everything was in perfect order, Nidia. You're right, that boy is very responsible; I never saw her house as orderly as that morning. But I didn't get to hear the man's voice on the phone—I was dying to know it! You were the one who had the luck to be there, you who don't even care about the matter. You have your mean side, don't you? Although I'll admit that every one of us sympathizes with people often without knowing why. And the same thing with dislikes, although now you're beginning to understand her better.

There in the airport she could give me more details. You were right: in front of you there at home she didn't say everything, but I don't think it was for lack of trust, it was just that she was tired after her first day back to work. Think that she took off only three days, after the ordeal of getting her stomach pumped. You were right: she had her tantrum on a

Friday night, Saturday she stayed in the hospital, but Monday when he went to her house everything happened. Again. Just as you suspected.

But don't be concerned, she's already gotten over her love fever, she didn't tell any lie in front of you, it was all as you heard it with your own ears, except for the main thing, of course, which was the tumble in the hay, to call it something. But afterward she was sorry for having given in, because she didn't feel a thing, she was frozen inside. She says, and you heard her, that his offense hurt her deeply and succeeded in killing whatever there was inside her.

What do you bet? That she'll get enthusiastic again or that little by little they'll stop seeing each other? I'll bet that little by little . . . she'll get enthusiastic again! I don't know why, but something tells me. I hope so, poor thing, and it's even possible that he might get to know her a little and learn to appreciate what she's worth. Yes, Nidia, she is good, convince yourself. Or maybe it's just the way I see her. I'm very fond of her, she has been very affectionate to me.

To think that at the end everything depended on you. If you hadn't told him the lie that she was coming back on Monday from São Paulo, he wouldn't have called again. It was a good idea, telling him that Monday she was coming back and that yes, she did have something urgent to tell him. Now, I don't know how she managed to justify the matter of the urgency. I forgot to ask her about that detail. Which was the main one. If she had a good excuse ready for having called him, then she'd maintain her womanly pride intact. But if she didn't have anything really urgent, aside from the desire to see him, she'd be shown up as a nag. How awful that role is.

But if she left that urgent message to call back immediately, she must have had some good excuse prepared, but what could it have been? I can't forgive myself for not having asked her. In any case, he returned and you earned her gratitude for as long as she lives. So, Nidia, maybe we'll call you before this letter reaches you. Have a little more patience and wait for me, I'm a little worn down, if not I'd get on the next plane and get to the bottom of this.

Ay, Nidia, how exasperating all this is, for the few damn

days of life left me I have to deal with this nonsense. Leaving my little garden in the Rio apartment is the worst, leaving those ferns behind, and those enormous leaves on the tiger-striped plant. And whoever's going to buy the apartment won't know how to take care of anything. I'd water them, and then from the bedroom window I'd see them shine and grow, getting more and more beautiful, light green and then deep green, without the slightest touch of yellow, giving forth some new bud, again light green. It's so beautiful to see things grow, raise themselves from the ground, but well anchored by their roots.

While we're on the subject, don't be fooled by the rain. Water regularly: some plants are well sheltered by the big branches on the palm tree and the raindrops don't manage to wet them thoroughly down to the ground—don't be guided by the rain, touch the soil to see if it's dry or not. Saying goodbye to each plant is going to be like dying each time, or feeling like they're going to die without my care. And my nice furniture, bought on that street with all the second-hand stuff. Lovely things, some real antiques. It will all have to be sold. And I'll mourn for each item sold. There's so little time for the final goodbye to this world that these other farewells don't make me the least bit happy, Nidia. I don't want any sort of goodbyes. I want to be at ease in my corner. That isn't here, where there's nobody I know or love. My corner is there in that little single bed, from where I can see the garden I myself planted six years ago. I don't have time to plant a new garden, especially in such a pretty but cold place as this. It was terrible enough to leave everything in Buenos Aires, but I was young then, I was seventy-five! A kid! Now I'm eighty-one and not a kid anymore.

Forgive me if I depress you with these things, you're eighty-three, and on top of it, what happened with Emilsen. I know, nothing that terrible ever happened to me, but I haven't gotten away with anything, either. It's better not to keep track of who's ahead on such matters. I don't want to talk about the ugly things in the past, nor do I want to lose all the nice things in the present. But that's life, Nidia, now the present is this exquisite city on the shores of a lake, and you can have it.

Now my little garden in Rio is a thing of the past, why deny it? How short a time things last. And how difficult it will be for us to see each other, because two hours or so by plane between Buenos Aires and Rio you can do without any problem, but thirteen or fourteen hours is something else. The ticket costs a fortune, and we can't stand the exhaustion any longer.

There was one thing I wasn't going to tell you, but I think it's better to prepare you for it. Nidia, you can't imagine what it is, I'll bet you haven't even the remotest idea. It's just that Ñato says I might not be returning at all to Rio, that he might go later on to close the house himself. That would be in case I didn't have the energy to deal with the strenuous round trip. Ay, Nidia, I really shouldn't be telling you these things.

And one of the things I'd most regret is that I wouldn't get to see the face or hear the "bottom of the well" voice of the neighbor's suitor. I'm dying of curiosity, Nidia. The photos I saw were so small that I couldn't get an exact idea of what he's like. Poor Silvia, I hope she has a little luck this time. All she needs to be is a little less pesky; that for a man is the worst thing, having to put up with a pesky woman.

Well, Nidia, I'll stop here because I'm very tired. It must be the heating, with the windows closed. Tomorrow Ñato will take it to his office and mail it from there. I don't have any post office nearby here, it's too long a walk. How I miss the neighborhood post office back there.

Love,
your sister Luci

What a coincidence! Last night just after I sealed the envelope, Silvia called; she must have already given you news of me, I hope. It's six in the morning, I keep waking up earlier and earlier; there in Rio at this hour the newspaper would arrive and I'd read it all the way through as the day began. Portuguese was so easy, and besides, there was always news from Argentina. Now I can't even read the newspaper.

Ñato is going to take the letter to his office and send it from there. What a pity that the neighbor didn't think of speaking to you before calling me, that way she could have given me fresh news of you. But that's how she is, she must have felt a sudden impulse and called me. That's how she is; she doesn't think about the expense. And here I want so much to talk to you and I don't dare waste money that way; one thinks differently, we were brought up another way, and in those years when it was worth the trouble to save a peso. Now with this inflation nobody can accumulate money for anything, which must be why people down there spend it like drunken sailors.

We were never like that, and besides, here the prices of things are so, but *so*, high that it sometimes makes me laugh. When I tore open the envelope to add these few lines I felt that I was wasting a fortune; you can't imagine what paper and envelopes cost! What garbage this Europe has become, so expensive.

I imagine that after hanging up she called you, to give you news of me. She didn't have much to tell, so don't think she's hiding anything from you. For the weekend she purposely accepted an invitation to go to the country, so she doesn't know if he called or not. But it seems to matter less to her, now that she has her feet on the ground again. You're going to kill me, but I forgot to ask her what excuse she gave him for her urgent call. Anyway it really seemed to me that she's beginning to get disillusioned. Her balloon popped.

I'm not a licensed psychologist, but it seems to me that she got so enthusiastic because at the beginning he needed her so much, and she was going to help him crawl out of that pit. That's the way she is; what she likes is to help people, and that's why she puts so much into her work. When things changed and he went out fishing on his own, it all crumbled for her. You think it was that? Time will tell.

Watch your diet, now that I'm not there to keep an eye on you.

Hugs and kisses,
Luci

One more thing. I reread this letter to see if there's anything I forgot to tell you, and I noticed that all I'm telling you are depressing things. One sometimes says things that one doesn't really feel; I'm not afraid to die, as it might seem in the letter.

I don't care if I die or not. I swear it. What makes me terribly
sad are goodbyes. I can't stand even one more. I think that
the ones who are afraid to die are those who believe in the
next world, because of Hell and all that. I don't believe; everything ends and that's it.

I can't imagine what more one could do in the afterlife. Be
sincere: would you or wouldn't you want there to be an afterlife? I don't think you would either; you were never able to
fool yourself with that; if not, you wouldn't have suffered so
much over Emilsen. Some can fool themselves; we can't. Of
course, seeing Mama again would be nice, but I swear to you
that deep down I don't believe in anything; I can't fantasize
that I'll hug Mama again. Life teaches you that you have to
accept the good things while they last, and not suffer when
they end. Mama was a good thing it was our luck to have, and
we should be happy that we had her. It's useless to hope for
impossible things; I think that doesn't help, at our age, what
do you think? Ciao again.

                              RIO DE JANEIRO, OCTOBER 15, 1987
Dear Luci:
    Today at lunchtime your letter arrived, but I won't get to
the post office this afternoon because, you'll remember, at five
they pick it up and it's already four. I almost skipped siesta
so that I could answer you more quickly, but I suddenly felt
so sleepy after lunch. I'm taking much better care of myself
than when you were here, because those back home in Buenos
Aires are furious that I'm alone here and don't want to return.
Their fear is that something will come over me at night and
nobody will be able to help me. I want to wait for you.
    They already called me twice; they couldn't believe I was
so determined to stay. They have a hard time accepting it;
they want me to come back no matter what. Luckily, Luci, I
have my independence, economic I mean, and I can do what
I want. I don't want to keep them holding their breath, but
they'll have to accept the situation. If winter were beginning
there they couldn't say anything to me, but now they can argue
that my main enemy, the cold season, has ended there. Don't

you worry about your plants; I'll take care of them till you return.

It's especially at night that I feel lonely, but I have no fear whatsoever, since this competent young man is a mere two steps away. His name is Ronaldo, and so far he hasn't let me down one single day; every afternoon he comes at six and accompanies me on my walk. He's very talkative, and I understand everything he says. He realized the difference between you and me, that you know much more Portuguese but you're as deaf as a doorknob and don't want to admit it. While I'm the opposite, my hearing is still sharp. Sometimes he talks fast and then I don't understand a word, but if he speaks slowly there's no problem. He's delighted to be earning these few cents, and I feel so pampered with my companion who takes me here and there.

I don't think his face is deceptive; he looks good and is good, he's already shown me pictures of his wife, a pretty, plump little girl, completely white, while you saw how dark he is. It's an odd thing, Luci, if you see him during the day he looks like a mulatto, with more black in him than anything else, but at night you notice his white features and it's as if his skin only seems dark because there's not enough light. I like those cute black faces, little round faces, but this one has another beauty, a finely chiseled oval shape. Because you'll have to admit, Luci, he's a gorgeous boy.

I already took note of the other assistants around, the one with the little old man in the wheelchair who we'd always see, the one with the old lady with the cane, and others, all with their impeccable nursing uniforms, but none like this one in looks. Of course he'd look great in a white uniform, but it's a big expense and who knows how long I'll stay. I don't feel at all like going, Luci. You're right that Rio is nice.

Look, Luci, what you said left me thinking about the afterlife. I don't know what to tell you; I never think about it, it doesn't even cross my mind. I think you're right, we have to be content with the good moments we've lived and that's it. Well, I don't know, I don't want to lie to you; deep down I seem to think just like you, but I can't put it into words.

Better to let me tell you more about this boy. I think that

his family's misfortunes have helped me to be more content
with my lot. He's a boy from the Northeast, the region that
had such a bad drought, remember? Or have you become completely European? Well, now it's raining again, but the whole
place is very poor, which is why all the doormen in Rio are
from there, and a lot of the maids. There's no work there. So
he and his wife came a few years ago, and he never found
work as a main doorman, with a dwelling in order to be with
his family. He was always just a janitor, those who wash the
floors and all the worst tasks, who don't get a dwelling, barely
a little corner in the cellar, where the other cleaning atten-
dants also sleep (if there's more than one), along with the night
porter during the day, and of course you can't bring anyone
to live there, a family member.

I mean that's why his wife was a maid in the building across
the way, where he couldn't sleep either, because there were
two maids who shared the room, her and the nursemaid. So
they lived two years like that, sleeping apart. And she was
allowed to go out at night but they didn't have money to pay
for a hotel, you see, so they led a life of sacrifice. And one fine
day she went back to the North—as they call it, not the Northeast. She went to live with his mother, in the country. And
he got tired of so many pails and soapy rags and worked as a
bricklayer for a while, and then later he became a night watchman since she wasn't there anyway for him to see at night.

They're paid the same, the one who works all day and the
one who sits doing nothing all night. And why? I asked him
and he didn't answer. But then he said, because of the danger!
At night there can be assaults and most of the time the watchman doesn't escape harm. Even when the watchman doesn't
offer resistance, sometimes the muggers kill him so that he
won't be there to identify them from the photos the police
would show him.

I know what you're thinking, that that expression on his
face when we come by at night is fear of assailants. But think
about it some and you'll realize that those are not fearful eyes.
Every time you talked about the eyes of the boyfriends of the
woman next door I thought of this boy, because ever since I
arrived in Rio he's left an impression on me, precisely because

of that. His eyes are so big, but always as if remembering something; what casts a shadow over them is some sad thought. His face is perfectly oval-shaped, a straight little nose—with that chiseled oval, there's not much space and his face is taken up by his eyes, and the shadow isn't cast by his eyelashes only. That's the strange part; where does that dark shadow come from? Oh, Luci, where if not from his sad thoughts? What else could it be! You don't need to reach eighty to have bad memories.

He hadn't told me clearly why his wife had gone back to the North; it's that she was pregnant. And there in her mother-in-law's house she had a baby girl. He stayed here. They didn't see each other for several months, until he couldn't stand anymore his longing to see the baby and he left the work he had, which at that time was washing floors and so forth. And he tried to survive with his mother's harvest; she has a little land. But it wasn't enough. And then came an epidemic of pneumonia, according to him. I'd never heard of such a thing, an epidemic of pneumonia; it's not contagious, is it? I don't know what he meant. The point is, the little baby girl, then over six months old, got sick on them and they took her to the hospital immediately, but nothing could be done, you understand? He then returned to Rio alone. I think it was all because of malnutrition. And since then he hasn't seen his wife, but she always writes to him, pretty handwriting, you should see, although I don't understand much.

And there he is at his post at night, watching the couples go by, and the families, and all those who have the joy of being together, and he doesn't have anything, not even a roof over his head or a bed to sleep in. That's the main problem with Silvia's building, that it only has the doorman's apartment, behind the garage, and for this poor boy there's nothing. Now guess where he sleeps. At the beginning he gave me vague explanations, but yesterday he finally told the truth: in a construction lot! We passed by the entrance and I couldn't believe it. It seems to be a construction that's been partly suspended for lack of funds, and they're doing something but not at full speed; the frame of the building is in place, up to the last floor. And that's where this poor thing sleeps during the day, while the others are working there—not very quietly, as you can imagine.

To think that one complains, having a whole apartment to do as one likes in. The big problem of these people is that: no roof, you see. So much misery in such a rich country! But worse is our misery, in the winter of Argentina. Well, I don't know if this letter will reach you before you come here; just in case, though, I'll mail it. You keep calm and get well, don't travel if you don't have the energy, I'm here getting along fine, the plants are watered and I always touch the soil—don't worry—to see if it's dry. Of course it shouldn't be like mud either, because then the roots will rot. So I'm telling you, take things easy since I'm not budging from here, even though those in Buenos Aires are pressuring me.

> Love and kisses from your big little sister,
> Nidia

ALFREDO MAZZARINI, 8 FRANZÖSISCHE STRASSE
LUCERNE, OCTOBER 21, 1987

Señora Silvia Bernabeu
Rua Igarapava 126
Rio de Janeiro

Dear Friend:

Sad circumstances lead me to write to you. I know that you and Mama had great affection for each other. It's hard for me to put this in writing, and to give you the news in this way. Mama passed away five days ago, last Monday the sixteenth, of a heart attack. The only positive part of this whole tragedy is that she didn't suffer at all; I don't think she had even realized the end was so near.

I had been with her all of Saturday and Sunday, and we decided to stay home because of the bad weather, wind and rains, and discuss everything we were so worried about; I'm referring, of course, to the move. Mama was very calm and decided not to keep the house in Rio, because she was already getting used to the idea of living in Switzerland.

Monday morning I got up at my usual hour, eight, to be at the office by nine-thirty, and Mama as usual was already up and had even had breakfast. Being almost ready to leave, I went to the kitchen to reheat the coffee I had taken too long to drink, and then I heard Mama say to me from her room that she had lain down because she was a little tired. I went to ask her what she was feeling, and she was already lifeless, stretched out, her hands as if caressing the pillow, totally serene.

The doctor, a neighbor, arrived very quickly, but I had already realized that Mama had left me. Forgive me, Silvia, that I didn't give you the news by phone; what follows will show you the complexity of our family situation and my reason for preferring this means of communication.

Nothing can be done for Mama now; no one knows that better than I. But there's also the delicate situation of my aunt Nidia, to whom we've decided not to break the news until she returns to Buenos Aires, if when you read this she hasn't yet gone back. When this happened to Mama, I of course got in touch with the relatives in Argentina, especially my cousin Eugenio, Nidia's son, and her son-in-law, Ignacio.

You must be aware of my aunt's health problems; the poor thing wanted to travel to Rio no matter what to be with Mama, against the doctors' advice, given her high blood pressure. But she insisted so strongly that they decided to support her in this plan, considering also that the Buenos Aires winter wasn't good for her. My poor aunt had suffered the loss of her daughter last year, and that made her seek Mama's company more than ever.

The fact is that this poor eighty-three-year-old lady finds herself (or found herself, because I hope she has returned) in a city where she doesn't even know the language, alone, and with the possibility that she might somehow learn of the death of her only sister. Her son called me in despair because when he spoke with her by telephone my aunt Nidia had roundly refused to return to Buenos Aires. Perhaps the excuse we gave her wasn't adequate: I suggested my cousin tell her that

Mama wouldn't return, that I would go to close the apartment in a few weeks, and consequently it wasn't worth it for her to wait alone in Rio. But her response was final, that she feels very well, and on her way to total recovery, as she put it, according to my cousin. Total recovery!

Knowing of your past kindness and concern, I'm informing you of the situation so that you'll lend us your support. We at least want you to know the truth so that you won't be left wondering about the situation. My cousin's hope is that my aunt will get overwhelmed by loneliness and decide to go back home, if she hasn't already done so. I think that's characteristic of her age, a certain initial stubbornness that later gives in to reason. The main excuse she gives is to take care of the plants in Mama's little garden.

Well, talking to you I'm already starting to feel better, to the point of being convinced that my aunt must be in Buenos Aires by the time you read this letter. Because the only logical explanation for my aunt's attitude is that she refuses to believe that Mama won't return to Rio, and that she keeps waiting for her because she simply doesn't accept the idea of losing her with the move to Switzerland. How much worse the reality is! But her son is very afraid of the emotional shock of her being told while she's alone in Rio, and he's considering as a last resort going to fetch her and telling her in person.

I'll simply close by sending you greetings and thanking you for any help you may be able to give. What's more, if any special problem comes up, please don't hesitate to call me collect at my office here, between nine and five, 239-5111.

Yours affectionately,
Alfredo Mazzarini

9

Dear Aunt Nidia:

How are you? We're having some problems here because Mama is still bedridden. That's why she's not writing to you, as I explained to you yesterday on the phone. Forgive me if I wasn't very talkative; it's just that your call caught me by surprise since there's now a difference of four hours between here and Brazil, and at that hour I was already sleeping. Besides, you must know that the rates from Brazil are very high, much more than if I call you from here. I didn't pass you to Mama, because she was sleeping and, on top of that, she's completely lost her voice, as I explained to you. In any case, it was a great joy to hear your voice on the phone, just as if you were calling from the corner, and to know that you're doing fine.

It makes me happy that Rio has been so good for your health, but I'm also worried because, as I explained to you, we've decided to close the apartment. After this initial setback to Mama's health she'll do just fine in this climate, the doctors assured her, and then I'll go back there to settle everything around Christmastime, taking advantage of the fact that the office will be closed for two weeks.

Mama asked me to tell you not to worry about the plants,

that unfortunately it's useless to wait for her, and that she's not writing to you because they've prescribed total rest. Both of us, she and I, are very worried that you're all alone there, so that we'll understand perfectly if you return immediately to Buenos Aires. What's more, we would feel easier if you did so as soon as possible.

If you have any practical problems, get in touch with my ex-secretary, Teresa, who is very efficient and can make reservations for you and would be glad to take you to the airport. Her office number is 511-1049; home, 287-8615.

Well, dear aunt, I have nothing more to say except to send you a big hug. If by New Year's I wind up everything rapidly in Rio, putting the apartment on sale and all that, I'll make a quick trip to Buenos Aires, where I hope to see you then.

Much love,
Your nephew Ñato

RIO, NOVEMBER 4, 1987

Dear Luci:

Yesterday I received your answer, or rather, Ñato's. How brief! It was over before I started. I hope your next one is double the length, because I'm savoring the joys of summer, waiting for your letter at noon, and when it arrives I'll sit in the garden, which is nice and cool because I watered it early, and in the shade of the palm tree I'm going to die laughing over your stories about the cold back there.

Tough luck! That's what you get for being so tied to your son. Tell him to go fly a kite! Be like me, I emancipated myself, as my youngest grandson puts it; he wants to emancipate himself from his older brothers. He's always saying that because he has to beg them to take him anywhere and they pay no attention to him because he's the youngest. He always tells me: Grandma, just watch, soon I'm going to emancipate myself.

A new paragraph for your blessed plants. They're doing fine: it rained and the leaves were thoroughly rinsed. As for me, my digestion is fine because since I'm alone, Luci, I cook

very little or nothing, though I do spend the whole day thinking of food. That's normal in a person with backed-up hunger.
And the one who's always bringing up the subject is the kid,
Ronaldo, who makes me laugh talking to me about food, because he wants to talk me into fixing one of those dishes from
up North, as he calls it, which seem very heavy on the stomach
to me. But he did get me to grill some fish, very healthful, as
long as you don't put any sauce on it, which you can add or
not, it's optional. Since it's so spicy.

But I know you must be wanting me to tell you about the
one next door; it came to mind because I wrote the word
"spicy" above. You can't imagine the news I have for you. I
hadn't laughed like that for a long time, when this kid told me
a few things that . . . well, I can already see the doubt on your
face, but in any case those things make me laugh, and they
must be true; why would the kid lie?

I'm laughing because we, especially you, were so concerned
about her loneliness. Now, this boy has come to confide in me
and he made me promise not to tell you, but way over there
you have nobody to gossip with, so I'll tell you about it without
the slightest remorse. Hold on tight: remember telling me
about two suitors she used to have? I'm talking about the
Argentine man who sold chemical products, and the surfer.

Well, Luci, it's not true that she stopped seeing them. They
come to visit her late at night! Not together, of course, that
would just be the limit. They come around every once in a
while, once every fifteen days or so. Ronaldo told me that one
was a surfer, so there's no doubt about that, and that the other
one has an accent like ours, and that he travels, and sometimes
he brings him something from the North, those sticky candies
they make there. Of course, since he comes so late, when the
night watchman is already half asleep, he ingratiates himself
with him by bringing something, like a tip.

According to this boy, those two never stopped coming; he
doesn't remember any long stretches when she didn't receive
one or the other. But since these suitors always appear very
late and nobody in the building sees them, she still has that
proper reputation. And I asked him if the men came just the
same when her son was there, and he told me she would go

downstairs and meet the surfer or the other one on the corner
and take a taxi—with the surfer, not the other one, because
he has his own car.

And where would they go? I asked Ronaldo, almost ab-
sentmindedly but thinking they would go to one of those fashionable bars, or to eat at some place that closes late. And the
kid told me they'd go to a hotel! Directly, he told me, even
though I don't believe he had any way of knowing for sure.
But that's the most likely.

And we two worried so about her. And that's not all; there's
another one who comes from time to time, but by the description he's Brazilian and of a pretty indefinite age, so he could
be anyone. I know what you're going to say, that it's that
Ferreira. But no! It's another one! Because this kid would
recognize Ferreira in an instant, and he never came after that
Monday when he appeared thanks to me. At least he didn't
come at night, and she didn't mention him anymore to me.
The kid never saw him but he knows because I described him,
bald and a bit potbellied.

The men never stay to sleep; they leave more or less two
hours after arriving, the kid figures. And the same thing when
they'd go out because her son was in town; she'd never return
after two in the morning. So there, Luci, I won the bet. I did
bet you anything she was loose; what a pity I didn't bet money,
because then I would have cleaned you out.

And that's not all. The day before yesterday she telephoned
to ask how I was, because I have to admit she's very attentive,
and I brought up the subject of Ferreira immediately, before
she could hang up. And she told me there was nothing, he
didn't call her anymore, and she'll always remember him but
she doesn't think of calling him, because it's clearly not going
to work. I was pretty daring and asked her why she thought
he was so withdrawn. And she gave a pretty deep sigh and
announced that something must be brewing, she feels there
might be a surprise soon; she feels it in the air, maybe a good
surprise.

If I get up the courage, I'm going to ask Ronaldo to find
out a little more about this mysterious other man. But let me
return to the conversation with the neighbor. She admitted

that when she starts to like someone a lot, but a lot, she always gets scared because she knows it's going to end badly. Even though, all the same, she does whatever she can to win the battle, she never gives up beforehand. Poor girl.

Forgive me for not having more news about her; as a matter of fact, she invited me to her house to chat but by that hour I'm feeling pretty tired. Now I'll explain it. I felt so upset about what this kid told me about his family in the North that to distract myself I bought some material and I'm sewing him a few things for his wife, poor thing. So between that and taking a walk with him in the afternoon, I don't have much fuel left in the tank and at night I feel sleepy. All this came about because the other day the boy had a terrible fight with the building manager and he wanted to go back to the North, leave it all. Apparently, he gave a rough answer to one of the owners and the manager demanded that he beg forgiveness and the boy refused.

He told me this when he came in the afternoon for our walk, and to say goodbye because he wanted to go back north already. Very few brains there, he barely has enough saved to pay his way! And not a cent to take to his wife and his mother. I then told him to explain everything to your Silvia, that she would know very well what kind of person the man was who had treated him insolently. No sooner said than done. Right away she explained to the manager that this scoundrel of a tenant, who's well known in the building for being nasty and overbearing, was very clearly at fault.

Well, when the kid was thinking about returning to the North it occurred to me that I could sew him something for the girl, but the truth is that he wouldn't have given me enough time. But luckily, everything worked out, and the kid's not going, and she might even be able to come here someday. Why not?

Well, tomorrow I'll write you a few more lines before going to the post office. One detail: it's getting hot and the leaves of the tiger plant start to bend if I don't give them a bit more water in the afternoon. Around five-thirty, before getting dressed for the walk, I give them their fresh water. Besides the usual one in the morning, of course. When I come back there they are again, standing up straight. Till tomorrow, when I'll add a line or two.

November 5. Last night there was a lot going on. They called from Buenos Aires very worried because I still haven't made plans to return. If they only knew that each day I feel less and less like going back there! It turns out that as Christmas approaches there won't be any plane seats available, and they want me to make a reservation for next week. But I'm no fool. Baby got very nervous and wanted to come here to get me if I was afraid to travel alone. But what worries them most is my being alone at night, in case something happens to me. So I promised to hire someone. I already had an idea, but first let me tell you about the second call last night. See how popular I am.

Well, I was annoyed by Baby's phone call, and ready to grab paper and pen and tell him a thing or two, when the phone rang. It was almost ten o'clock at night, so I first thought of you, of course, but immediately figured that it would be two in the morning there. So it had better not be you, because no one picks up the phone at two in the morning to give good news. The second person I thought of was Ferreira, but it wasn't him either. It was your Silvia!

She was a little down and was calling me to talk for a while. As she seemed a bit insistent, I went over; she sent Ronaldo to accompany me and afterward the sweet boy brought me back home. Oh, how sorry I feel for that boy, sitting there all night in that little entrance hallway. I feel sorrier for him than for the psychologist, or maybe not, she too is an unfortunate creature.

So here it is: she called me because she felt alone; she says that sometimes an attack of despair comes over her, but that now she's starting to see things more clearly. More than anything, she misses her son and now she's getting used to the idea that he'll never return permanently. And now listen to this: she told me that she's seeing her earlier suitors again, she admitted it. And that she's realizing it's much more practical at her age, and for her profession, to see people that way, without having to get heavily involved. Though at one moment she sat there staring at me and came out with something odd: that she was just saying these things, but what if he came back and suggested a complete turnaround in their lives? At that point she could do anything. Because he had come to have such great power over her.

But in general she seemed fine (and this morning she probably woke up in even better spirits because we had talked). I was already quite sleepy when the phone rang; she answered in Portuguese, so it was either the surfer or the one we don't know, and quite clearly they were planning to meet in a little while. Then I had to go back home, out of discretion, without making clear what I wanted to ask her about: whether she could recommend some girl she knew, some maid in her building or ours, to hire to come sleep here. As long as you have nothing against it, of course.

The truth is, I wasn't thinking of taking on anybody for the moment. Later on, yes, but after Baby's call I decided to give them at least that satisfaction, of knowing that I was accompanied at night. And now I'm going to tell you something that makes me very happy, and it's that I thought of this marvelous idea. Look, Luci, you are going to sell the apartment, or rather, rent it, while you check out how things are going in Switzerland. What could be better than to rent it to me? Because this climate is very good for me. And I thought that the boy next door could bring his wife and they could live comfortably in the next room, which I never think of going into, now that you're not here; every evening you and I watched some movie there.

I brought the television into our room, not the VCR, because this way I'm forced to watch and to practice my Portuguese. Luckily, I haven't lost my hearing, and let me tell you that each day I understand more. That way I also have a little more to talk about if I meet up with someone, because all the ladies here watch the evening soap operas. I speak to them in Spanish, but they understand everything I say; the same with the boy, though I'm not embarrassed with him and I say any silly old thing in Portuguese.

But with his wife I would like to be able to speak a little better, so that we could have nice long talks. I always forget to ask him if she does that needlework they do in the North, those embroideries! It would be great if she could teach me how to do that knitting that's so difficult; on TV they did a short thing on how they stick a pile of needles into a kind of ball of wool, and out of that they gradually make the design, so beautiful. And I understood that program of current events quite well.

Oh, but how silly I am, you were the one who told me to learn Portuguese by watching a little television. I didn't want to know anything about it, remember? It's just that on my first trips here I felt intimidated by the new language. Anyway, I don't use that other room, so they can make do with it to sleep in, they don't even have to buy a bed, with that sofa there that turns into a double bed. The only thing needed would be another nice blanket. There's enough for two people, but not for three.

I haven't said anything to the boy yet, so as not to get his hopes up until it's a sure thing. That's why I'm sending you this letter. I'm asking your permission to bring her, her and the boy, to live here. But I'm also suggesting that I rent the apartment, or buy it from you. I don't have ready cash at this moment, but I can sell the apartment I'm renting out in Buenos Aires, and so what if I lose out a little in the transaction? The main thing is one's health.

What else? See what a long letter this is, so you send me one just like it, though you probably won't have much news, now that you can't go out in the cold. Don't worry about the stamps, since they send it from Ñato's office. Let those multinational businesses be useful for something. I forgot: last night when the boy accompanied me back home, I asked him if he knew some reliable girl in the building. And he told me right away: not in his building, but in ours, there's a nanny who has to sleep in the same little room with the real maid, and you've seen how tiny those servants' rooms are.

He doesn't know the nanny, or rather, he's never spoken to her, but he heard through somebody else that she's newly arrived from the country. The boy doesn't know the other girl either, the maid, so he's not sure if they're uncomfortable in that little room. Maybe her employers make her sleep in the living room with the baby, who knows? But I'm waiting until nine o'clock, a sensible hour in the morning, to go ask the baby's mother if she wouldn't accept an arrangement like that.

What more could she want than to be relieved of one person at night? Because these apartments are not so big, for you and me they're fine, but for a family with kids and maid and nanny it's utter madness. I'll even offer to give the girl dinner; when the wife comes home from work she must want the baby in her arms all the time anyway. And the nanny is probably more in the way than anything else.

But this would only be a temporary arrangement. What I really want is for the boy's wife, whose name is Wilma, to come down from the North. The boy showed me her letters, she seems like a saintly person, poor little thing.

Oh, Luci, last night we stayed up talking a long time; that boy breaks my heart. Because when you're with him there's nothing sad about him, he's the life of the party. Those sad eyes he gets when he's alone. And he's convinced—just listen to this—that he's very lucky in life, and on the street when we see some beggar or a drunkard, or tramps, both sexes, men and women, he always feels that life has given him a lot. I don't say anything to him, I let him talk, because at times I think he's pulling my leg, but he's not, he really means what he's saying. For example, he keeps telling me now how great his father was, and his mother, who's still living, I already told you that. Not his father though, he died some time ago, and that's when all the hard times began.

The father was the village barber and the mother a cook on a kind of ranch, a few miles from there. Both of them worked and they had all they needed. Especially children—boy, do these people have children! And Ronaldo was one of the youngest. And I think the mother was the real dynamo in that home, because he says she would get back in the evening and still make their dinner and then do some sewing, what a saint! The boy loves her a lot, but I think he loved the father even more. He says everyone in the village still remembers him without being resigned to his death.

Because he was such a vital man, and the organizer of the kids' football championships, and of all the sports contests and

parties, and he'd make fun of anyone he caught off guard, and
Ronaldo adored him, as all the other kids did. But the father
wasn't very happy with this child, because he was a poor
student at school. And I asked why he had disappointed his
father in that way, and the boy told me in all sincerity, and
his eyes filled with tears, that he couldn't sit still at that age,
he always had to be doing something, jumping, running, that
he couldn't just sit on the bench because he'd get ants in his
pants, and that's why he'd run away to play leapfrog, or play
ball, because he had that, ants in his pants. Or the devil inside
him.

And the mother would save all she could, she didn't want
to buy ready-made clothes, she'd make the father's shirts, and
little shorts for the smaller kids, because with the heat that's
all they'd wear. I told all that to Silvia, talking about this boy
I felt so sorry for, who had nothing in life, and she then explained a lot of things to me about Brazil, which had made
plenty of progress for years, before the military destroyed
everything as they did back home, you know, and people saved
and fought to have their things in life, just like back home,
remember? And during that period it was worth the trouble
to save because there wasn't that inflation we have now and
people were optimistic about progress.

And everything in that house was pure joy. And work—
needless to say—but work with hope; you understand what I
mean, because more or less the same thing happened in Argentina. That's why, according to Silvia, this boy is somewhat
a product of that era, kids nowadays aren't like that, this one
is already twenty-seven, so he managed to have a whiff of
better times, and deep down he thinks the future will get
better, and he knew the warmth of home life, and that's why
I think he doesn't lose hope about building one.

Now, what happened with the father is terrible, he died of
a brief illness and then everything started going bad. This boy
was not yet a young man, the most delicate age, when he
suffered that loss. And then the most incredible part: the
mother let some man into the house, to take the place of the
father. She was inconsolable, it appears, and this coincided
with the beginning of the drought, and the ranch was left

without farmhands, and she lost her work as a cook, and she let this man come into the house, who was some kind of bricklayer, or builder of some sort. And one by one the children started leaving to work elsewhere, because the drought was serious and, worst of all, this man was the worst possible stepfather. Not that he bossed them around, but he always insisted on silence and never let them play the radio or anything, and at eight o'clock he'd go to bed and there had to be total silence. And he didn't talk to the kids at all, not even to say good morning or goodnight.

But with the mother he was a bastard. The kids weren't sure if he beat her, but more than once they'd come home and find something broken, because the man threw things against the wall to let off steam! And they'd find the mother crying, and always with her back covered up, which is where these types prefer to beat their wives, the boy told me. And according to him, the other people on their block think the same thing about this man, that the farther away you are from him, the better.

Yet with all that, the boy still considers that he has a lot in life. It must be because he doesn't lose hope of seeing good times again, he adores his wife, and if all turns out well it won't be too long before she's here. Maybe he realizes he's found someone ready to help him, although I don't say a thing to him, and that's why his spirits are so high when we chat.

He really is a bundle of joy, this boy. He always has something to tell me, he likes to talk about food more than anything else, and about his wife, who he says is the prettiest and best girl in the world, so he has to be thankful to God for sending him that girl after giving him the best parents in the world. And he also adores his oldest sister, the one who in a sense finished bringing him up, because she took him into her house when that stepfather began ruining everything.

But I wanted to explain to you clearly why this boy is the way he is, and I can't find the right words. His joy is contagious. It must be because of the teeth—you'll say I'm crazy—but he has perfect white teeth and he smiles at the drop of a hat; that mouth of a young, healthy boy gives off who knows what, a kind of light, with his immaculate teeth and nice full lips with that healthy color, that stretch to his ears when he smiles.

Yesterday we sat on one of those benches at the beach to chat a little in peace, and as I sat there gazing at him for a while it seemed like he was changing; he spoke to me of the dances they had in his village, and how he began to court his wife, who was never alone, always with a female relative, and it seemed that he was getting more and more handsome, that the light he gives off from within was growing, that it wasn't a person who was speaking, with so much affection for the beauty of those times, which would come again because he was blessed with a good life, and he looked like an angel, Luci, not a mere boy. I was really struck by this. I'm no madwoman, Luci, I'm not the kind to see visions, but I swear to you on the memory of Emilsen, for me the most sacred thing in this life, that the boy was transformed as he spoke, he was no longer just another dark kid, which is what he is, he was a being from another world.

But how can he be so content, when at six in the morning he leaves that little hallway that's like a jail, without ventilation on any side, and has to go home to that construction site? He already showed it to me! I insisted so much that he took me; I wasn't going to tell you, because you'd say I was crazy. And there were some workers there and he didn't want to go in, but I told them I wanted to see how the construction was going, that I was interested in buying an apartment, and they let me do a thorough inspection!

What I wanted to see was where the beds were, what nook or cranny he slept in, and I almost died, because it's in a corner of the basement, where the garage is going to be, and the floor is covered with papers and rags. Some of the others have a mattress, and some don't even have that, it's a place where not even rats would stay.

At first he was very ashamed of the others, but afterward we continued the "tour de luxe," to quote those good-for-nothing thieves at the travel agency who charged us forty dollars for that little tour of the hills of Rio. He even showed me, with great pride, that he does have a mattress. He found it on the street one night while crossing the square, the one facing the post office. And he carried it all the way to the construction site, about ten blocks. But the thing is, he's very handy; he showed me how he'd rolled it and carried it on his head, and there you go. I then told him I didn't believe him, because he never goes by that little square at night. And then he confessed that he had been going out with a little maid around there, but that he doesn't see her anymore. Rather naughty, right?—being married and all. But with his youth and all this sea air, you can imagine how hot the poor boy's blood must get.

And afterward he made me go up I don't know how many stories to show me where he fixes his food. No, we were already up there, because he and another trespasser hide from the engineer up there to nap. Well, with some bricks he's built a stove, and he lights up coals inside. Stove! Barely a little brick box. Well, I don't think I'm making myself clear: he put some bricks on one side and some on the other, forming a square. And lying next to it was an empty beer bottle, which he uses to crush those black beans, and a package of the mandatory rice. He and that other one eat separately, another man who isn't with the construction crew either but who they let sleep there. It seems they all get along fine.

According to this Ronaldo, poor thing, there are two kinds of construction sites, the ones that have a night watchman and the ones that don't. Where there's a night watchman there are always fights because the engineers make him comply with orders not to do this and that during off-hours, and everybody is always in a bad mood. While at smaller sites like this one, where they have a low budget and can't pay a night watchman, everybody feels more at ease, after work hours everything is peaceful because there's no stool pigeon telling everything to the engineer.

So it seems that they stick together. One of them got drunk one Sunday and attacked Ronaldo with a broken bottle and they all defended him and the man felt ashamed and left. They say he was a good man but that the liquor made him bad, changed him into someone else. Let's hope he doesn't appear in the little hallway of the building next door, with a broken bottle; there's nothing easier to get hold of.

I'm afraid for him in that job, exposed all night to any riffraff that might attack the building. But I think that once he has a place to sleep he won't have trouble finding another job, during the day. Though on the other hand I like the idea of him working at night, so that his wife can stay up talking to me until bedtime.

Well, it's almost nine. I'll go talk to the nanny's employer before she goes to work. Then I'll take a leisurely walk to the post office.

Lots of love to Ñato; thank him for his short note, and write soon and at length.

Love from your sister and future tenant, don't dare say no!

Ciao,
Nidia

RIO, NOVEMBER 4, 1987

Dear Baby:

It was a pleasure to hear your voice yesterday. I noticed you were a little angry with me, and I hope you're getting over it.

First of all, here's some good news for you: starting tonight a girl is coming here to sleep over. She seems very nice; she works as a nanny in this building, and I've just proposed this arrangement to her employer. The woman immediately jumped on it, delighted, and right then and there called over the nanny and explained to her in good Portuguese what I wanted.

The girl went wild with joy because she's going to earn a few more cruzados and she's going to sleep in a bed. Guess where she was sleeping? On a mattress on the kitchen floor. Because the tiny servants' room only has space for one cot, and a very narrow one at that, for the maid. I already knew how the servants' quarters are in this building.

So rest easy about me being accompanied at night. The girl is very young, fourteen years old, although she already looks

like a young lady, a beauty, quite dark, with very light green
eyes that make for a wonderful contrast with her skin. But
you really don't know this girl's coloring; it's not that pretty
dusky color of the Argentine brunettes, no, it's more like the
suntan the Argentine girls get at Mar del Plata that makes
them look like ripe fruit, bursting with health. But this girl
has this color naturally, because if not you'd immediately notice the tan lines.

Well, dear, let's talk seriously now. You can't imagine how
surprised I am by this turnaround of my health. It feels like
another life. It doesn't even feel like myself. And one's health
is priceless. So I'm going to make a proposition.

Don't get all panicky, since it is a rather drastic decision. I
want to stay here and I'm going to stay here. I'm doing it for
you. Because if I return and anything bad happens to me,
you're the one who will feel guilty.

I already wrote to Luci asking her as a great favor that she
rent the apartment to me. I'm really the one doing her the
favor. Besides this girl who's going to sleep here, I've already
hired a very serious fellow, who works as a night watchman
in the building next door, to take me for a long walk every
afternoon, so that I'm following the doctor's orders about taking walks.

From tomorrow on, that fellow is also going to take me
shopping once a week to the street market. For me it's like
going to a party—so many colorful fruits and vegetables!—
not to mention the flower stands, which belong on a postcard.
They set it up once a week, from early morning till noon. Luci
and I would go all the time and find a boy right there at the
market, which is very crowded, waiting to carry things for
the old ladies, and for the not-so-old ladies too, because the
packages can sure pile up.

But I'd rather go with this fellow, who I can trust, and who
needs to earn something. Later on I'd like a woman to accompany me to the market and to the supermarket, because
they're more patient; I already have one in mind. But that's
for later on; for the moment this fellow is a good solution. The
little nanny couldn't go to the market with me at that hour,

with the baby to take care of. Aside from all that, of course, the cleaning woman still comes twice a week for several hours, to tidy up the house as when Luci was here. So you see I'm getting the best care, and besides, the help here is good and cheap.

Now for something more serious: if Luci needs to sell this apartment because she has to buy a place in Lucerne, or whatever, I want to buy it. Think about what would be the best way to handle this matter, if it can be done by taking out some money I have invested in our business, or if it's necessary to sell the apartment on Irala Street. I'll let you choose how to do it. But I definitely want to secure the apartment, no question of that. It's a whim, the only one I've allowed myself in my whole life, always at the service of saving and watching over the household economy. But my health, I think, is worth the trouble.

In any case, it's an excellent investment; property in Rio is always going to have value; it's a very desirable place.

Well, I've given you enough news for today; love to your family, and to Ignacio and to Emilsen's children. How is Ignacio doing? Before, the idea that he'd set up a home again seemed to me like a sacrilege, an unforgivable offense to Emilsen's memory, but now I'm thinking it's the best thing he could do, poor boy. He should wait a little, though, right? One is still in the blossom of youth at fifty, so there's no hurry; he should be very careful who he gets involved with.

Think that at that age I too was left a widow. But it's not the same for a woman, and the times were different. But the truth is, it never even occurred to me to marry again. For me your father was the only man who existed, and nobody could take his place.

I'm pestering you too much, so I'm going to take a slow walk to the post office, with my beautiful parasol, just in case the sun is beating down hard. But back to Ignacio. The kids are already grown; the only one left is the youngest, who's still in short pants, but before you know it he too will be a man, and what will poor Ignacio do all alone? You must understand that very well, because your daughter is already a doctor and it's been a while since she's had any time for you or for her grandmother. That's life; when I married I too began to see less of Mama, poor thing.

                                                    Love,
                                                    Your Mama

P.S.: My dear son, promise me that you'll never again call me in such anger. I must tell you that you got quite insolent. Don't do it anymore, because afterward I feel crushed. In over fifty years we've never fought; a fine thing that would be to break up now, at this stage of the game.

One more thing. Tell me the truth, that middle-aged woman you mention so often, who goes to your house so much, is there anything between her and Ignacio? Don't hide anything from me; that would only be worse. Besides, I'll understand.

10

Silvia Bernabeu
Rua Igarapava 126
Rio de Janeiro
November 12, 1987

Señor Alfredo Mazzarini
8 Französische Strasse
Lucerne

Dear Friend:

I truly appreciate your trust in writing to me concerning
your aunt. Not to mention my great sorrow over dear Luci.
It's best not even to get into that, she meant so much to me,
a touch of Argentina next door to my house, a true refuge.
They say that opposites attract, and her romanticism was a
balm to me since I'm the other extreme and needed that different vision of things. By "romanticism" I mean an attitude
toward life which revolves around emotions and imagination
as opposed to rationality.

Señora Nidia is so different, on the other hand, so practical
and with her feet on the ground. With her there's not much
dialogue because she says the same things that come to my
mind; we're too much alike to be interested in each other.

If I were you I wouldn't worry too much about her; maybe we should take a lesson from Nidia. I don't know if you will like what I'm going to say, but I support her will to independence. Her son will probably not look kindly upon my attitude, but the circumstances of the case leave me no doubt about the legitimacy of such determination. To begin with, I am convinced that dear Luci's absence would not invalidate Nidia's plans. She now has other emotional ties.

I've been wanting to write you this letter for days, and what stopped me was that I wasn't totally convinced of what I would say to you. But this afternoon your aunt came over to ask me to translate into Portuguese a letter to her future companion, and she left with me the pages in Spanish. I think that the best I can do to make you understand what Nidia is currently feeling is to transcribe that text for you. I don't think I'll be doing anything wrong, revealing something intimate without the third party's authorization. In my opinion the end, in this kind of long-distance professional consultation which we are involved in, justifies the means.

Dear Wilma: I'm writing to you directly to thank you for the greetings you sent me in your letter to your husband. Pardon my familiarity, but at my age I've gotten used to that, since all of you seem like children compared to me. In a few months I'll be eighty-four.

Believe me if I tell you I already know you quite well from the photographs and all that Ronaldo tells me. I hope to be assured soon that I can rent my sister's apartment, so that we can send you the ticket for that horrible two-and-a-half-day bus trip. If I had more money I'd send you the airfare. Which is not totally out of the question.

It's just that I'm very worried that you're so crestfallen, that you might be crying in some corner every afternoon, I know too well what that's like! I too lost my daughter, almost two years ago, and I don't have my husband beside me either, to give me strength. I lost him so many years ago. But you, dear, you haven't lost yours. He's here enjoying good health and waiting for you; he always talks about you, it's clear that he loves you immensely.

Have faith that everything will work out fine, and soon you'll be with him, and not like the last time, sleeping with another maid in a room not big enough for one. Your room here is very pretty, it's not a servants' room, because my sister turned that into a closet, you don't know how vain she is! She's two years younger than me, but she's a miserable old lady all the same, and spends her time buying clothes and looking in the mirror to fix herself up, and the truth is, she knows how to improve her looks.

I, on the other hand, have no patience with getting dressed up, you'll see, but don't be scared away, I don't go around looking like a witch. My daughter Emilsen always scolded me about that, and she'd always make Luci the example; Luci's the name of that crazy old woman who's my sister. When you're here I promise that I'll fix myself up more; Emilsen used to like me to use curlers during the day so that my hair would be more fluffy in the evening, and if you help out every morning I'm going to tie on those damn curlers. Luci couldn't because she has arthritis in her fingers; all she could do was to pass the comb through my hair, which did tidy it up a bit.

So you see, that would be one of your jobs, to help me to be better groomed, since I don't want Emilsen to see me from somewhere and be frightened. That's a silly thing for me to say, since I don't believe in the other world. I wish I could. It would give me another consolation. I hope that you do believe, so that you'll have that illusion of someday meeting your little daughter again.

Let's talk about something else, since things are sad enough there up north. I have to congratulate you on your husband, because besides being so handsome he's very affectionate. Old people realize that better than anybody, because nobody looks at us; they don't realize that with our experience we can understand the problems of young people and do something to help them. And there's nothing shameful about needing help; we all need something from others, and too often we don't dare say it.

Well, there are people who don't need anything from others, what they do need is time. That's the case of my grandchildren, whom I adore, what healthy children, three boys and a grown girl! But they all have so much to study that it's been years since they've given me anything but an affectionate kiss. I realize how much they love me, but as I was saying, aside from that kiss they don't give me anything because the poor things are preparing for life's struggle and have their noses stuck in textbooks the whole day long.

My granddaughter is the eldest, she already has a doctor's degree, and she still keeps studying, so she can specialize. When her aunt died, my Emilsen, that same afternoon she had to go to her job at the hospital. She couldn't even cry one tear in peace for her aunt, what a hectic existence. Is that a life for a woman? It does so much good to relieve oneself and cry a little.

I'm telling you this because I think you should know that nobody gets away with anything. We two, you and I, have plenty of time to cry over our dead ones, at least we can permit ourselves that luxury. See what foolish consolation I'm offering you?

Well, I won't continue, because this letter has to be translated into Portuguese by another very busy lady who's going to just die when she sees the time I make her waste.

Pray that everything will come out all right, I hope to see you soon in Rio.

                         A warm hug from Nidia de Angelis de Marra

So, back to our conversation. If Nidia ever asked me for advice, which she hasn't done so far because she knows very well what she wants, I wouldn't hesitate to support her idea of settling down in Rio. I have only one reservation, which isn't easy to explain in a few words. This boy Ronaldo is very odd. I haven't had extensive dealings with him but I've been able to see, from his attitude in general, and from Nidia's stories, that he's a bit on the childish side.

Contact with him has been good for your aunt, since his cheery personality keeps her laughing. She's very struck by the fact that the boy is so optimistic, when his life has been a real disaster area. I've noticed that the boy has sudden down moments when he's forced to confront reality, and at those

moments he gets very violent, like a baby, violent in an ir-
rational way, and highly self-destructive. Here's an example:
the president of the tenants' association one day criticized a
shirt he had on during work hours, when his night shift was
just about to end, without knowing, that pompous imbecile,
that the kid had still not received the spare shirt that the
association itself is supposed to provide. Well, right there and
then poor Ronaldo tore off his own shirt and went off angry,
with his own shirt in shreds.

Knowing a little about the boy's history, I think we're deal-
ing with an emotional development arrested at age twelve,
when his life changed radically upon his father's death. Much
of Ronaldo's great vitality doubtless has neurotic roots; he
doesn't want to accept that the happy circumstances of his
childhood (a certain lower-middle-class well-being in addition
to the love of an exemplary father and mother) have changed
in such a negative way.

But if we're going to seek someone free of neurosis to es-
tablish whatever relationship, we run the risk of spending our
whole life carrying Diogenes' lantern. Neither should we put
ourselves in the hands of totally irresponsible people, but
sometimes those who appear so well balanced can give the
wisest of us a nasty surprise.

I hope to have news from you soon; I'm always at your
service for any consultation; in a way you keep me close to
Luci, whom I miss so much.

Warmest good wishes,
Silvia Bernabeu

LUCERNE, NOVEMBER 19, 1987

Dear Aunt Nidia:

We've just received your letter. This is only a short note
so rest easy about that. Mama is not getting better, I wish I
could tell you otherwise.

I'm going to Rio, taking advantage of Christmas vacation.
I will arrive around the 20th, and if I can wrap things up
quickly I will be with you all on the 24th in Buenos Aires. It's

difficult for me to comment on your plans, the ideal thing would be for you to go to Buenos Aires for the holidays, and after talking things over you could return to Rio, if that is your wish. Now by letter it's difficult to answer all your questions about the apartment.

Keep in mind that it wouldn't be very good for you to spend Christmas alone. I hope we see each other in Buenos Aires.

Love,
Ñato

RIO, NOVEMBER 25, 1987

Dear Luci:

I've just received a letter from your son. It seems to me that Switzerland is not doing either of you any good. You're down with something and he seems so mysterious and gloomy. What's going wrong over there?

The worst of it is that he's leaving you alone for Christmas and New Year's. Has that boy gone crazy? Please don't show him this letter, poor Ñato! He was always so good to me, and always treated me with so much trust; why's he being so roundabout now? If he has some other plan for the apartment, he ought to tell me so right away, because then I'll start looking for another one.

Imagine what an arduous task that would be. And I wouldn't only be looking for the place. Tell him that in general nobody pays a thing for used furniture, so I would still be the ideal customer. A fine mess that would be, to have to start looking for furniture. And curtains. And some little rug. And don't tell me you're going to sell even the bedclothes! There you must need different blankets, bedspreads, everything, to go with the new beds. Speaking of blankets, I don't think there are enough here, for two people yes, but not for three. If you're thinking of bringing me a little gift from Switzerland, that would be the most practical, a nice cheery colorful blanket for me to use. And I'll give the regular ones to the couple.

I almost had a fit when I got that letter, I'll tell you. I want to be here for Christmas. I'm already making arrangements for Ronaldo's wife to arrive around that time. Oh, Luci, she wrote me such a wonderful letter; I'm not sending it to you, because I want to keep it and sometimes things get lost in the mail, so I don't want to risk it. I'd copy it out for you, but since it's in Portuguese, it would take me a year.

Every night the girl I spoke to you about comes over to sleep. She's a good soul but too quiet; you have to yank words out of her with a corkscrew. What she likes to do is watch the TV soaps and movies. I fall asleep and she takes the television into her room and continues watching. But she doesn't have much to say; I've tried to bring up subjects but got tired of doing it. Wilma, it seems, will be different, just from her letter I can tell that she's more communicative. Besides, this one's a child, thirteen years old! Though she looks like eighteen.

But how inconsiderate I am, there you are with health problems and it's up to me to lift your spirits a little. I have the best remedy, gossip!—which you like better than food, it seems. Besides, it's gossip about none other than your neighbor Silvia. And her number-one boyfriend.

Well, fasten your seat belt, there's turbulence ahead, as they announce on the plane. It all came out of her own mouth when I went to visit her so that she could translate for me the letter from Ronaldo's wife, whose name is Wilma, or did I already mention that? I can understand the newspaper in Portuguese, but with that handwriting I couldn't manage to decipher even half the words. But if they're from the North and know how to read and write, that's already a lot.

Well, let's get back to what you're most interested in. I have to confess to you that Ronaldo had already informed me that the notorious fellow had been there the night before, so that I also went with the hidden intention of finding something out. What a good sister I am, eh? She brought up the subject of Ferreira all on her own. She dared call him again! What gall that woman has. According to her, she wanted to prove to herself that she could deal with him now with a certain distance and not lose her head over him once again. So she called him and the man came and told her, guess what, that he's having a serious relationship with another woman. Can you imagine that? Doesn't that hit you like a ton of bricks? Forgive me for not giving you fair warning.

She's a single girl, forty-eight years old, with whom he had already had a long relationship. It seems that he initiated her in these matters; I'm using the neighbor's words—I didn't dare ask her to explain what she meant—and that's why he felt a kind of duty to look her up again. He knew her when he was single, and initiated her, how do you like the word the psychologist used? And he didn't marry her but the other one. And that poor devil of a girl never again saw any other man, she was left buried alive, and sometimes he'd call her and they'd get together. This goody-goody is a high school math teacher.

So the wife had been two-timed for ages. But some time ago, long before she got sick, the wife caught wind of it, and so the man stopped seeing the goody-goody. But he always regretted having ruined the goody-goody's life, since she never had a home or kids, all for love of him; I'm starting to think he must have some charm for more than one woman to lose her head over him. But charm, my eye! That balding scoundrel, it's just that these women get themselves all wound up over nothing, like this one next door.

And finally it came out why he had disappeared after such a lovely trip to the island. A sudden impulse struck him and he almost turned his back on everything and went off to be a sailor in a fishing boat. What do you think of that? But keeping in mind his children, who still need his economic help, he held himself back. But it seems he had a hard time of it, and went for weeks without seeing anybody. And what I don't know is how he met up with the goody-goody again, if it was he who called her or if the devil fixed it for them to run into each other on the street.

I think he was foolish, because with the one next door he would have had some economic support, you know this woman never stops working, Luci, these psychologists earn so much! She's about to buy another apartment, she told me because I said I wanted to find out about prices, just in case you two don't rent or sell me this one. And she's up to date on all the prices, of course, because she's about to make a sound investment, so what do you think of our suicidal friend?

Now, for what follows I hope that you at least give me a medal, I think I deserve it. Knowing how curious you are, before going back home I asked your neighbor point-blank: if this last time with Ferreira anything happened or not. I had the nerve to ask her! Did you think me capable? You wouldn't have dared.

And the answer was yes. This girl isn't so finicky with me, you know; she treats me more like a friend, whereas she respects you more, like a mother, I think.

The truth is, I've never seen her in better shape. She's delighted with the direction things have taken. She gave the whole thing a self-serving interpretation that I can't agree with at all. I'll tell you: according to her, the week on the island for that man shook him up, awakened his dormant desire for freedom, for the adventurous life of a young man, and she became a symbol of all that. So that on their return he suddenly rejected her because she was a kind of challenge, she meant the possibility of a radical change. And since he didn't dare leave everything once and for all to live a free life, that's why he couldn't face her anymore.

I'll go on with her interpretation, following her words as closely as possible, which you must recognize by now: the reason why the other woman came into the picture again has to do with a class issue, the fact that she's petit bourgeois, words that your neighbor likes to use a lot, but she looks the other way when she says them, I realized. Does she think I'm an idiot? She must consider me petit bourgeois too and doesn't want to point the finger at me.

And so doesn't she charge an arm and a leg for therapy? She'd better not put on the leftist act for me, because I'll get mad. If I'm petit bourgeois, she is too, a little bit more of a trollop, of course, but she likes money all the same. Well, I'm getting off the subject. So her version is that the guy must have gone looking for the goody-goody to take the place of his deceased wife. And at that point she always uses another word, which I never remember. In one ear, out the other.

But then why is your neighbor so pleased? Because now,

according to her, she has the role of the mistress, the third side of the triangle, which is the best role, with the least commitment, and from her position she's going to continue to help him resolve his problems. Oh, now I remember the little word she uses! According to her, the goody-goody doesn't "question" him, while she does. Understand what I mean? The other one, she says, doesn't question him, in the sense that she doesn't stir things up inside, doesn't force him to confront himself.

Look, Luci, as far as I'm concerned these are all excuses she invents so as not to accept the bitter truth. In love things aren't so complicated; if you like someone a lot you forget about all the reasons and advantages. What advantages is she talking about? If you fall in love for real the advantage is being with the other person who made you lose your head, and that's it. Advantages . . .

What happened is that she fell in love with him and he didn't fall in love with her. Period. There was something about her he couldn't quite swallow, and that's it. Now, what he feels for the goody-goody, who knows? But one thing that's clear, he did not fall in love with your neighbor. Although I will admit one thing, him I don't understand. She's an interesting woman, no beauty, but she has her charms, and besides she doesn't mind picking up the tab! I don't understand that man.

Well, now I have something very harsh to tell you. You're going to get a little frightened, but I was so shocked that I have to tell someone. It turns out that this poor boy Ronaldo is becoming very attached to me, and he tells me everything; I did wrong to ask him certain questions, and now he tells me everything, as if he were at confession. Well, I'll take this one step at a time, so as not to give you a stroke. As it happens, I always felt sorry for those bricklayers sitting at the door of construction sites in the evening, all of them short and kind of ugly, and I'd ask myself, why? Do they pick them as dwarves because they're stronger?

Then I asked him and he told me they're almost all from the North, where people are shorter. He's not, you already saw. Bricklayers work so hard and are so badly paid; that's why nobody does it but these poor things dying of hunger who have fled the drought. And then most of them are far away from their families and sleep there at the construction site to save as much as possible and they carry that deep sadness inside, since they miss their loved ones so much. And their little huts in the North must be miserable, I imagine, but mansions compared to these cockroach dens where they sleep here.

But you remember all this. The new thing I want to tell you is something else. At one point I told him that those poor things lived like monks. And then out came the story. He says that at that site there's no night watchman, so they're all in agreement not to tell anything to the architect, etcetera. They all go to sleep after dinner very early, at eight, and one of them always stands guard, and around midnight, when the neighborhood is completely deserted, women start to visit. They're usually young maids, also from the North, who feel very lonely, and they duck out from where they work, or ask permission, who knows? And some of the bricklayers have their steady visitor, and others who are more timid or ugly don't get anything, and must wait for a maid to appear who doesn't mind going with more than one man, what do you think of that?

That happens on weekdays but not on Saturdays; the girls who have a steady boyfriend don't want to go near the site on Saturday night, because there's lots of drinking and rough-housing. Other women come on Saturdays. Some of them, it seems, come from very faraway neighborhoods; those who don't have a steady boyfriend, they're older, I don't know, women already beaten down by life, who can't come on week-days, because of the cost of transportation, sometimes they have to take two or even three buses, and they're sick with sadness, from the North too, and stay there the whole night, and are passed from hand to hand.

But that happens only if another woman doesn't see them. The men hide them, they don't let these women be seen by the others, because if there's another woman present they want to stay with just one man the whole night. But usually on Saturdays only one or two come by, and the men give them a little of that aquavit, that cachaça that I like so much with lemon. And that poor girl lets her tears flow, and talks about home there far away, and then continues drinking and she goes from crying to laughing. And the men win her over with pretty words, and don't even give her a cent for the bus back. Because as soon as the buses begin running again, at around five in the morning, which is already daylight in the summer, the woman has to risk going out and being seen by someone. This boy says it's difficult to make them leave, they don't want to, because they're very sleepy, and have drunk so much and slept so little, but the men take them out like bags of garbage to be hauled away.

He worked many months at that site, when they began construction. That's why he became friends with all of them and they've let him sleep there during the day since he began working as a night watchman here next door. So he turns out to be some innocent boy, eh? And that's not all: he often leaves his post and goes to the site because some girl is waiting for him on the corner. Around three in the morning, if everybody living in the building has come back to sleep. And if somebody is still out, this you're not going to believe, he has the girl come in, and hides her in the machine room, in the basement, a disgraceful thing to do.

And I saw the place! Last night when I came downstairs from Silvia's house he was in his little hallway, of course, and as I was dying of curiosity to see the basement I asked him to take me. You enter by the garage, you go down a short little staircase because it's not even a basement, it's like, I don't know what, a shed with a low roof where the elevator motor is, which hasn't been working for some time. And there the janitor keeps the cleaning equipment, which is why there's not even anyplace to spread a sheet of newspaper for a woman to lie down on, and he prefers to go to the site. I'm repeating this no-good kid's words, isn't he simply outrageous?

Once the girl is down there, he feels at ease because he won't let her leave until the last of the tenants has come back from carousing. And then after a while he goes down there. So he's not to be trusted, that's why the wife had better come soon, before he gets into some mess.

I'll continue tomorrow, because the nanny arrived; I'm going to ask her to help me fold the sheets. Yes, without ironing, I know you disapprove. But as far as I'm concerned, stretching them out on your pretty patio leaves them looking ironed enough.

Luci, here I am with Silvia, she came over to visit. She found out from Ronaldo that this morning I bumped into something. I didn't tell you, so that you wouldn't worry. Well, I'll tell you later. After a lot of insisting Silvia agreed to translate into Spanish and dictate to me Wilma's letter, because I want you to read it. Here goes:

Today the 26th. It's very early in the morning, the girl is still sleeping, I woke up with a little pain in my leg, from the bump. I'm writing to you on the kitchen stool where, strange as it seems, it's least painful for me to sit. Last night your neighbor was going to dictate the letter to me and when she was beginning, I don't know what came over her; she was so struck by what Wilma said that I couldn't get her to dictate anything. I'm going to copy it all for you myself in Spanish, I think that will be easier. It begins like this:

My dear Señora Nidia:

Here my mother-in-law and I are in good health, thank God. Ronaldo writes very little, but he has already told me that the señora is very good to him.

I hope that God gives the señora everything she deserves. I would ask one thing from the Holy Virgin for the señora, that he bring back to life her little daughter who died. I would ask the Virgin the same thing for me; that's why I know what the señora has, stuck in her heart, a long knife that everyone wants to help her take out, but it keeps sinking deeper in. As we know, sometimes the Holy Virgin performs miracles, and I'll ask her to let you have the first miracle, señora, since you're old. And while we're waiting for the miracle I close my eyes often and manage to see my little baby.

The señora tells me that she doesn't think she's going to see her daughter anymore, why does she say that? God is going to get angry if He finds out. When I'm very sad, and I'm suddenly afraid that my husband will go off with another woman, I cry a little, which makes me very tired, and I close my eyes and see my little baby, always cute and healthy, as before she got ill. But sometimes I see her ill, and right there and then I open my eyes and run off into the fields. I get afraid that in the next world she'll continue suffering as in the hospital.

But I barely ever see her that way, she's almost always pretty and chubby. And if I can see her in this world just by closing my eyes, it will be even easier to see her in the next. There I want to hug and kiss her, and give her her little bath, and comb her hair. Often Ronaldo's mother lets me serve the food, and I take advantage of this to give my mother-in-law much more. And if I eat only a little I get weak and sleep badly, but that's good for closing my eyes and seeing the baby. But for that it was even better when Ronaldo was here, because he'd climb on top of me in the morning, and at night, and in the evening when he'd come back from working in the fields, because he says he loves me so much, and also because he wanted to forget about sad things. But he's very healthy and doesn't get weak, and I give him a lot to eat, and since I'd be so tired I'd see my baby at all hours when Ronaldo was here, all I needed to do was to close my eyes a little.

My mother-in-law hasn't had her eyeglasses for months, and she doesn't see much. That's how I can put more on her plate. It's just that here we are without work, and the little that we harvest we already sold, and we spend that money only a little at a time, but with inflation it loses its value, and here there is no bank, we have to go to the next town, and a man told me that the bank is no help either. I take advantage of the fact that she doesn't know what's going on and there are mornings when I wake up already sad, especially if I get to thinking that Ronaldo is going off with some other girl, one of those who spend all their salaries on bikinis.

He's very handsome and here all the girls were after him,

but he chose me because I never let him touch me and he knew I would be a good mother for his children. So when I wake up sad I want to cry to make it all go away, but I can't close my eyes because then I see my little baby suffering, and those days I don't eat anything, and my mother-in-law doesn't realize it. When she had her glasses she'd shout at me and make me eat; she has a very strong voice, she's good at shouting. But when she's being absentminded and I eat almost nothing in the afternoon I start feeling something in my chest and I tell my mother-in-law that I'm going out to hunt down a bird with the sling, and I go out when it's almost dark and I cry a lot. And afterward I feel very weak and I sit under a tree, and closing my eyes I see some beautiful things, Ronaldo comes walking toward me, and we talk about having another child, and he makes me a child and I have it and it's just like the baby girl who died, I don't know if it's a girl or a boy, it must be another girl, because it's just like the first one.

Ronaldo doesn't want me to talk about things his mother is going through, but it's good that you know. That man is not in this house anymore, but she feels sorry for him and goes to take care of him sometimes. He still works when he can, but they don't give him as much work as they used to. He lives alone, all his children went off to Rio, and my mother-in-law goes and prepares his food. Ronaldo doesn't want me to say this, but that man helps out my mother-in-law with a little money, but sometimes his nerves go bad. He was the one who broke my mother-in-law's glasses, my mother-in-law says she dropped them on the floor and he stepped on them without meaning to. I don't believe her.

My mother-in-law should go live with her daughter who's in Recife, not the one in São Paulo, because of the bad situation there. She stays here because I'm here, that's what she says. I think it's because she feels sorry for the man. Ronaldo has to write and tell her to go to Ana Lúcia in Recife. It doesn't matter if I've left by the time the letter arrives, she has good friends who can read her the letter.

Many many good wishes to you, señora, and may God

help us all to be together soon. Many hugs and very re-
spectfully yours,

Wilma

What do you think of the letter? I think she must be as
good as gold. But there are always surprises. In any case,
without trying you get nowhere. And I've always believed
that if we can do a good deed, it's our obligation to do so.

Well, I don't receive a letter from my sister but I do from
a poor soul I don't even know. From Buenos Aires nobody
writes, they pick up the telephone and with that they fix everything. But on the telephone one is nervous and doesn't say
the main things. If Emilsen were alive, it would be another
matter entirely. I had some bad thoughts this morning, so I
looked for your last letter. I never answered what you asked
me, if I could hope that someday I'd meet again all our loved
ones who have died. I can't, Luci, you're right. If you never
could, you who were more fanciful, then certainly not me. But
you see these ignorant people from the North, how they manage to settle for that. Maybe it's their poverty more than their
ignorance. Since they've got nothing at all, they have no choice
but to invent those illusions. I envy Wilma that.

I told Ronaldo what she told me, although I didn't show him
the letter. And he too believes in the other world. I told him
I didn't, and he looked at me as if I were the devil in person
and he crossed himself! It seems he had never before spoken
to a nonbeliever, as we are. And then he began to tell me that
someone had wanted to do me harm, putting those ideas in
my head. To calm him down I told him that I'm too old to
have a head for certain things, and he told me he knows very
well how the other world is.

I swear to you, Luci, that he spoke to me in all seriousness.
He says he knows all about it, that first in a room there's his
dead father, but completely alive, cutting someone's hair, and
when Ronaldo dies he's first going to visit his father for a
while, and then in another room is the baby, who's being taken
care of by the Virgin and the angels, until he or Wilma dies
and can take care of her. And then he says there's another
room, where he's going to be waiting for Wilma until she dies.

Last night I couldn't sleep, thinking about all that. How lucky these ignorant people are. How nice to get to that first room, can you imagine? I'd like us two to be there as when we were young girls, waiting for Mama. I don't know if you remember, it happened very seldom, but sometimes Mama left us alone the whole day to go take care of some sick person. And as we weren't used to her being away we missed her like crazy the whole day, we couldn't live without her. And when she'd come back at sundown, there was that great joy in hugging and kissing her, and knowing that she'd stay with us forever. Forever, Luci.

And in the other room? I'm the same as Ronaldo in that sense, in the other room I'd like to have Emilsen, but as a little girl, she was so adorable then, that way there'd be many years to go, forty and more, before she'd get sick and leave me. Though in heaven there shouldn't be any more separations. And the worst, as you say, are the goodbyes. And in the third room would be Emilsen's children, also as kids, and wait, what I don't know is where I'd meet Tito, I swear I don't know. I must not want him to see me like this, because he's not going to recognize me, eighty-three years old, all bent over and bowlegged, with almost no hair left.

When Tito died I was barely forty, slim, with a nice straight back. And I don't want to see him as he was at the end, poor thing, all skin and bones, and in so much pain from that horrible disease. I want to see him as he was when I had just met him, and we danced so many pasodobles and tangos and waltzes. What a man. I just thought of that pleated dress, the pink one with the cream-colored jabot, and sleeveless. What a scandal I caused with that dress! Because it was sleeveless! It must have been around 1923 or '24.

I remembered something else, Luci. When the letter arrived from our relatives in Italy, that awful one, and Mama couldn't get up out of bed from so much suffering. They had killed Uncle Anténore, Mama's youngest brother, in Salonika, in the war. I think he was twenty-five. If the war was from 1914 to '18 that must have happened around '16 or '17, because I recall it wasn't near the end. It's been seventy years or more, Luci, and I remember as if it were yesterday. Do you remember?

Mama couldn't accept it, because she wasn't a believer either. And for us when someone is gone, it's forever.

And what if Ronaldo were right and we weren't? How nice to think that when Mama left this world, after such a long and painful illness, she met Anténore, and they could chat about everything they couldn't put into a letter, her in Buenos Aires, and him in Piacenza. A month away by boat. A letter would take a month and a half to arrive, and the answer would take another month and a half. Poor Mama. But she had us.

Well, Luci, this letter is going to cost me a fortune in stamps, I don't have a multinational company handy, like someone I know. But I just have to talk to someone, forgive me if I tell you silly or sad things, a good thing I'm sending along some tasty gossip to round it out.

Don't hide anything from me, you and Ñato, tell me things plain and clear. I can't wait till Wilma comes! Take good care of yourself.

Love and kisses,
Nidia

P.S.: Don't forget the blanket; if you don't come, have Ñato bring it to me.

11

Dear Mom:

You're right to ask me for a letter, instead of spending money on telephone calls. You've always had your head screwed on straight, and we'll hope that's the case this time too, with your revolutionary idea about emigrating. Do you realize, Mom, that you'd be emigrating?

I spoke on the phone with Ñato, he called from his office in Lucerne, don't panic, I didn't call him. So the company paid. He confirmed that he's going to Rio around December 20th, taking advantage of the official holidays. He doesn't see any problem with your renting or buying the apartment. He has to travel in any case to take care of business at the company branch in Rio, which most probably will be closing. It seems he always knew that and didn't want to tell Aunt Luci until the matter was decided.

When he arrives you'll have a long conversation and he'll update you on everything, so that you'll be able to realize clearly where you stand. The only thing I can tell you ahead of time is that Aunt Luci is never going to return, because Ñato is going to settle there in Switzerland. That's why you should think things over carefully, and plan out your future in Rio without counting on Aunt Luci at all. We're going to miss you a lot, but it makes us happy to know that you're much better, and that your blood pressure has improved so significantly. We're also relieved to know that Ñato will be with you for Christmas.

Mom, I'm so tired I can't keep my eyes open, I'm going to bed. Take good care of yourself, don't eat too much, your daughter-in-law here says you shouldn't walk in the sun without the parasol she gave you. Kisses from your son,

Baby

COUNTY CLERK / POLICE DEPARTMENT
Leblon Precinct–Rua Humberto de Campos 315

Statement of Incident

Today at 6:20 P.M., Wednesday, December 16, 1987, the following claim was made. Senhor Otávio Pedro Oliveira da Cunha, 22 years old, able to read and write, identification card no. 6087 registered at the Police Department of the State of Minas Gerais, maintenance worker in the apartment building at General Venancio Flores 119, neighborhood of Leblon, declares that his sister Maria José Oliveira da Cunha, a minor, has disappeared from her place of employment, at Igarapava 120, apartment 205. The minor performed domestic duties, principally as a nursemaid. Her exact age has not been determined, because the claimant does not remember her date of birth. He maintains that she is only thirteen, while her employer in apartment 205 informed the police in a telephone interview that the girl declared herself to be fourteen years of age. This lady identified herself as Nieves Castro Athaide and will appear to make a statement tomorrow. She has been summoned for a hearing at 6:30 P.M.

The minor Maria José also worked as a companion for another resident of the same building, in whose apartment, no. 104, she slept every night, as a principal part of her task. The employer is Senhora Nidia María de Angelis Marra, native of Argentina, who will make a statement tomorrow. She has been summoned for a hearing at 7:00 P.M.

The parents of Maria José and Otávio Pedro reside in the town of Parilá, Province of Minas, and according to the claimant have not received any recent communication from their daughter. The aforementioned have no telephone in their home, but the claimant communicated with them by means of the public telephone station in the town of Parilá, today at 5:30 P.M., immediately before appearing at this precinct.

Questioned about his conjectures regarding the whereabouts of the minor, Otávio Pedro seemed at one moment determined to speak, but suddenly he stopped, as if fearing something. He explained only that he was responsible to his parents for Maria José's behavior in Rio, since he himself had insisted that she move here.

He has resided in this city since his release from the army, two years ago, after serving his time as a conscript in the Second Artillery Battalion, stationed in Ribeira Preta, Province of Minas Gerais. He has worked in the same building since then, and several months ago, according to him after last Carnaval, he brought his sister to Rio because Senhora Nieves de Castro Athaide was going to have a baby and needed a nursemaid. Senhora Nieves is the daughter of a resident of the building where Otávio Pedro works.

This statement is hereby recorded before the undersigned, witnesses Sergeant Lucio Freitas Coelho and Police Lieutenant Arnoldo Campos Galvão, today, December 16, 1987, who countersign below with the claimant.

COUNTY CLERK / POLICE DEPARTMENT
Leblon Precinct–Rua Humberto de Campos 315

Declaration by Witness

Today at 6:45 P.M., Thursday, December 17, 1987, the following statement was made. Senhora Nieves de Castro Athaide, 26 years of age, teacher of English at the Anglo-Brazilian Institute, identification card no. 90.187-8 in the Province of Rio, states that the minor Maria José did not appear for work yesterday at her usual hour, eight o'clock in the morning. The night before, the minor had gone over as usual to apartment no. 104 in the same building, when Senhora Nieves returned from her classes, at 6:30 P.M., and could take charge of her baby.

On Tuesday, that is, the day before yesterday, Senhora Nieves had come home as usual to have lunch, and found the minor crying. Maria José did not want to explain but soon admitted that she was pregnant and feared her brother's reaction. Her employer tried to calm her, promising to inquire about the legality of an abortion for a minor. The minor then reacted vehemently, stating that she wanted to bear that child because it was all she would have left of the one who had taken away her virginity and whom she would wait for her whole life if necessary, without ever seeing another man in this world. Given the girl's generally reserved and shy nature, what most surprised Senhora Nieves was the deep love she declared for a man whose name she refused to give.

Since the previous month, when she began sleeping in apartment 104, she had taken her few belongings, so that Senhora Nieves had no information about the disappearance of the minor until yesterday, when she went to apartment 104, after 8:00 A.M., searching for the nursemaid. It was then that the resident of 104 informed her that she had just noticed the absence of the girl and her belongings. Both decided not to let the brother know until midday, when Senhora Nieves returned from work. The lady in 104 remained in charge of Senhora Nieves's baby.

Back at midday, having no further news of the minor, Senhora Nieves called her mother and asked her to inform Otávio Pedro, an assistant janitor in the building.

Senhora Nieves has not received further news of the minor and states that she has no further information to give. Testimony taken today, December 17, 1987, by Sergeant Lucio Freitas Coelho and Captain Luiz Carlos Araújo, who countersign below with the deponent.

COUNTY CLERK / POLICE DEPARTMENT
Leblon Precinct–Rua Humberto de Campos 315

Declaration by Witness

Today at 7:15 P.M., December 17, 1987, the following state-ment was made. Senhora Nidia María de Angelis Marra, native of Argentina, passport no. 9.471/5, tourist visa shortly to be renewed January 9, 1988, according to information put forth by the interested party, 83 years of age, states that she had not been notified by the minor of any intention to abandon her work. Senhora Nidia María adds that the minor's behavior was entirely proper during the few weeks when the latter kept her company and that there is no explanation for her disappearance.

The news of the pregnancy was communicated to her by Senhora Nieves, and the minor had never made any remarks to her about relations with members of the opposite sex. In any case, those who record this testimony observed that the lady was visibly nervous and that she contradicted herself upon being questioned about the possible disappearance of objects of value or money from her apartment. At first she said that nothing was missing and that it was unnecessary to inspect anything. But she later stated that she had inspected everything and nothing was missing.

The lady asked to be excused, due to her advanced age, and closed her deposition, adding that as the minor was very re-served, she had been unable to come to know her more inti-mately, nor was she interested in being notified of any information concerning the girl's whereabouts. The lady seemed seriously offended by the minor's behavior. Testimony taken today, December 17, 1987, by Sergeant Lucio Freitas Coelho and Captain Luiz Carlos Araújo, who countersign below with the deponent.

Silvia Bernabeu
Rua Igarapava 126
Rio de Janeiro

December 19, 1987

Señor Alfredo Mazzarini
c/o Thyssen Metal Co.
Calle Mariano Moreno 760
Buenos Aires

Dear Friend:
    Given that you didn't call me yesterday, I imagine that you
must have succeeded in changing your plane reservation to
fly direct from Switzerland to Buenos Aires. I hope that despite the deplorable mail service at this time of year my letter
arrives. As if this family matter weren't complicated enough,
it has come up during the New Year's holidays, with their
infinite snags. And I say "family" seriously, because for me
Luci was and continues being family.
    I hope that your telephone bill isn't too onerous, but since
you had insisted repeatedly I considered it necessary to call
you collect yesterday first thing in the morning. I don't have
much to add along general lines, but I can give you all the
details which by telephone would have seemed absurd to enu-
merate.
    I feel satisfied at having communicated to you the latest
events in time for you to have changed your plans and reversed
the order of your stopovers, first Buenos Aires and not Rio
as you had planned. I'm glad also that I will be gone during
Christmas but will be here the first days of January, when
you pass through. This at least turned out for the best.
    These are days filled with surprises, and one is that I'm
going to spend seven days with my son in Mexico; miracu-
lously, I got a reservation, the same way you probably did,
because of last-minute cancellations. What happens is that
people make these reservations so far in advance that when
the date arrives their whole life can have changed. Besides,
I'm paying business class, a fortune, but this Christmas I want
to celebrate.
    I beg you not to forget to call me when you come to Rio in
January, so that we can get together; I want to know all the
details about Luci's last days. This may sound like useless
wallowing in pain, but it's not that; what's worse for me is not
knowing the facts, which leads the way to flights of imagination

that aren't always positive. There's nothing like confronting the truth when we're trying to resign ourselves to an irretrievable loss.

But I'm getting away from the real purpose of this letter, which is to give you information about your aunt Nidia. Until three days ago everything seemed to be going as well as could be. Your aunt went every day to the very out-of-the-way Rio Bus Terminal to see if there was a refunded ticket or a cancellation so that Ronaldo's wife could make the trip. Given that the dates were around Christmastime, there wasn't a single seat until after the 25th. She then decided to have her come by plane, where there were no vacant seats either, although airlines, unlike bus companies, at least allow these matters to be resolved by a phone call.

Besides, that terminal is more than an hour away from our neighborhood, which did not keep Nidia from going every morning in hopes of a cancellation, and stand in line for hours, uselessly waiting. Finally a travel agency called her; they had secured her a seat on a plane for the 20th, and she had to come pay for it within forty-eight hours. Since I'm always eager for dollars, I changed them for her and she gave the money to Ronaldo to go pick up the receipt at the agency near here in Ipanema.

That was about a week ago and everything appeared to proceed normally. Last Wednesday night, the 16th, Nidia telephoned me, deeply alarmed. Ronaldo had not come by at six in the evening for their usual walk, and neither was he attending to his watchman's duties in my building, where he comes in at nine at night. It was already ten-thirty by then. And there was something else: that morning the girl who was her nighttime companion had disappeared from her house, without saying a word, and with her few pieces of clothing. Nidia asked me to accompany her to the construction site where Ronaldo slept during the day, but I had visitors and couldn't satisfy her request.

The next morning Nidia went alone to the site and spoke with a friend of Ronaldo's. He told her the boy had left Rio early Wednesday morning, because he had been accused of deflowering a minor and the girl's brother was looking for him to kill him. Ronaldo's friend didn't want to say where he had run away to, but when Nidia suggested that she wanted to send Ronaldo money the friend said that he was probably in the outskirts of São Paulo, where one of his sisters lives. But nobody knew the address. Finally Nidia took out a thousand-cruzado-bill and left it for Ronaldo, in case he appeared. The friend then said that he didn't want to hold on to the money, because Ronaldo would not be coming back, since he had left with the girl. Nidia insisted and left him the thousand cruzados.

She returned to her apartment and telephoned the travel agency to cancel the reservation. She then found out that Ronaldo had never gone by to pay for his wife's ticket, invalidated three days before. When Nidia had asked Ronaldo for the receipt he claimed he had left it somewhere, and the detail was forgotten. That same afternoon she was called to the police station of our precinct; she gave her statement within a few minutes and they didn't bother her with any questions.

Returning from the police station, your aunt was struck by a shiver of horror: the room where the girl slept had closets crammed full of nice things and a bureau filled with Luci's clothing. Also things of value. None of the jewels were missing, but the white lace dress was, the expensive one you had bought your mother on a trip to Fortaleza, completely hand-embroidered. And the white lace mantilla, I think from Spain, and what dear Luci valued the most, lacework from Brussels, I didn't understand clearly from your aunt what it was, a kind of shawl, also a gift from you to your mother, who adored embroidery so much. You must remember what it was. She didn't tell me the color, but all embroidery from Brussels is white, so that garment must have been white too. Luci had put it all away together, with a special wrapping to protect it well.

And in the same place she found a note from Ronaldo. I didn't get to see it, but according to Nidia he begged forgiveness and assured her that he didn't understand why he had fallen into temptation, when his great desire was for his wife to come. But he had to escape to save his life.

Nidia was especially disturbed by the stolen money intended

for the plane ticket, and the next day, Friday, she was already
back in Buenos Aires. She wanted to fly immediately; she left
the doorman a tip to water the plants, and the whole matter
of getting to the airport she arranged with your ex-secretary.
All this happened during work hours for me, and so I could
barely give her a hug between patients, just before she left
in the taxi for the airport.

She then told me something terrible: she felt guilty about
what had happened to the poor girl, Maria José, because she
had failed to protect her and warn her about Ronaldo. It's just
that she had never thought the boy capable of taking advantage of a pure and innocent little thing. Only then was she
realizing that her son was right, that she was of no age for
such wild enterprises. Poor Nidia was really in a state, and I
had no time to help her in that sense, to make her see that
she had acted marvelously well.

But all that was talked about on the sidewalk, in front of
the taxi driver, who was watching the clock, and me with my
patient waiting in the office. Since you'll see her in Buenos
Aires, I beg of you, try to show her that side of things but,
of course, without telling her that I told you to, since our
correspondence has taken place behind her back.

Your aunt Nidia did what she ought to, always with gen-
erosity; make her see that side of things, please.

What's left to tell you? I've talked to the janitor in dear
Luci's building, asking him to pass along the light, gas, and
telephone bills to me. Since you're coming in January I won't
worry about anything else.

While I'm still in Rio, every two or three days I'll look in
on the plants, just in case the doorman forgets to water them.
He knows me and lets me have the key without any problem.
Luci would suffer if she knew they lacked water. I'm off to
Mexico on the 22nd.

I imagine that by this time Nidia must already know the
truth about her sister. What a Christmas holiday awaits her,
poor Nidia! So thrilled as she was with her new family in Rio.
Sometimes I can't understand how people put up with so much
pain and disillusionment.

I look forward to seeing you here, and please, if you don't come here at least give me a quick phone call from Buenos Aires.

Best wishes,
Silvia Bernabeu

COUNTY CLERK / POLICE DEPARTMENT
Leblon Precinct–Rua Humberto de Campos 315

Statement of Incident

Today at 11:00 A.M., the 21st of December, the following statement was made. Senhor Orlando Lima Brandão, 45 years of age, identification card no. 101.658 issued by the Police Department of the State of Rio de Janeiro, a civil engineer licensed by the government of this city, overseer of the construction site at Sambaiba 198, states that during the night his personnel have been bothered by visits from Otávio Pedro Oliveira da Cunha, employed as a maintenance worker in the apartment building at Venancio Flores 119, in this same neighborhood of Leblon.

Otávio Pedro has appeared there searching for an individual who allegedly sleeps at the construction site, and who he claims deflowered his sister, a minor. He has appeared twice during the last weekend, first in a friendly manner and then in a drunken state, having come to brandish a firearm, with which he threatened anyone who refused to tell him where he could find the individual he was seeking. Testimony taken today, December 21, 1987, by Sergeant Lucio Freitas Coelho and Captain Luiz Carlos Araújo, who countersign below with the deponent.

COUNTY CLERK / POLICE DEPARTMENT
Leblon Precinct–Rua Humberto de Campos 315

Statement by Accused / Disorderly Conduct

Today at 6:00 P.M., the 21st of December, the following statement was made. Otávio Pedro Oliveira da Cunha, 22 years of age, able to read and write, identification card no. 6.087 issued by the Police Department of the State of Minas Gerais, employed as a maintenance worker in the apartment building at Venancio Flores 119, admits having appeared at the construction site at Sambaiba 198 in search of the individual who he says deflowered his sister Maria José Oliveira da Cunha, a minor.

Otávio Pedro then related the following events. A week ago, without being able to specify which day, his sister visited him at work and, crying, told him that she had believed in a young man's false promises of marriage and had surrendered to him. Her menses was already delayed several days, and the hospital examination had detected pregnancy. She immediately asked her brother to confront the individual, named Ronaldo Rodrigues do Nascimento, night watchman in the building situated at Igarapava 100, Upper Leblon. The minor incited her brother to threaten the culprit with death until he obtained a promise of marriage. Otávio Pedro did so, on Monday, December 14, but the night watchman denied all charges.

Otávio Pedro then threatened to come by the next night at the same hour, armed with a gun, if the watchman failed to go see him at his workplace during daytime hours, with the minor, determined to make amends.

On Tuesday the 15th Otávio Pedro awaited the visit of the night watchman but the latter did not arrive, so that night he appeared at the doorman's post in the building on Igarapava. Since the night watchman was not at work, he went to the construction site, sure of finding him there.

The watchman's cohorts let Otávio Pedro come in to verify his absence. The next day, Wednesday the 16th, Otávio Pedro also found out that his sister had disappeared from her employment, and he reported the incident to this precinct. Having no concrete proof against the night watchman, Otávio Pedro made no reference to him in the aforementioned statement.

The lack of evidence notwithstanding, two days later, without news of the minor and goaded by alcohol, he came by the construction site at night, exhibiting a revolver and threatening those present in the place, who had no information to give him about the missing man.

After this episode, Otávio Pedro affirms having thought over all that happened, and having understood the situation better, based on the observations of his fiancée, who will also make a statement about the case. Otávio Pedro affirms that he will not harbor plans for aggression, and swears under oath not to remove from the building where he works the firearm, property of the tenants' association, which he used in order to intimidate the workers at the site.

Statement by Witness

Today at 6:30 P.M., Monday the 21st of December, the following statement was made. Antonia Maria da Silva Lopes, 21 years of age, unable to read or write, identification card no. 57.983 issued by the Police Department of the State of Pernambuco, domestic servant at apartment 205 in the building at Igarapava 120, engaged to be married to Otávio Pedro Oliveira da Cunha, who recommended her for this job to the owner of the apartment, Nieves de Castro Athaide, two years ago, when Senhora Nieves entered wedlock and left her mother's house, in the building where Otávio Pedro works.

Antonia Maria cried convulsively as she began to talk, because she says she is incensed by the attitude of the minor Maria José, whose reprehensible behavior has resulted in problems with the law upon the person of Otávio Pedro. Antonia Maria met Maria José ten months ago, when the latter arrived in Rio to take charge of Senhora Nieves's newborn infant. Shortly after arriving, Maria José developed an intense feeling for the night watchman in the neighboring building, with whom she had no opportunity to speak because he only

appeared at late hours when the minor was unable to leave
the house on her own.

In any case, at some moment they managed to exchange a
few words and the guard invited her to visit him late at night
at his post. Antonia Maria, the present deponent, maintained
herself from the beginning in a state of vigilance, and even
took the key ring off the service entrance every night, leaving
it on a shelf in her room. But early one morning, at three
o'clock, she noticed that the minor was dressing to go out and
attempting to get hold of the key ring. She prevented her from
doing so, threatening to tell her brother if the incident occurred again, and she slept from then on with the key ring
under her pillow.

Late at night the minor would turn on the kitchen light,
where she slept on a mattress which was put away in the
morning, and the light would awaken Antonia Maria. The
minor pled nerves and insomnia, and would read magazines
for hours until she managed to fall asleep. On one occasion
she was discovered by Senhora Nieves, who forbade her to
turn on the kitchen light so as not to disturb Antonia Maria,
who sleeps in the adjacent room, separated from the kitchen
by a mere archway.

Antonia Maria from then on would sometimes find her late
at night sitting on her mattress in total darkness, unable to
sleep, because she would hear the minor going to the refrigerator for water. According to Antonia Maria, the minor never
cried in her presence, unless she was watching a television
soap opera, but she did seem obsessed with thoughts of the
night watchman a few steps away. Antonia Maria knew that
the watchman was married, and even remembered his wife
from when she had worked as a domestic in the neighborhood,
some two years back. Therefore she told the minor but did
not manage in the least to change her attitude.

What tormented the minor and what she spoke of inces-
santly was the possibility that another woman might succeed
in catching the individual with some scheme. Antonia Maria
questioned her about just what such schemes were but got no
explanation out of her. The minor affirmed that she would kill
herself if another woman were to take away the night watch-

man's love, and she lived in an evident state of anguish, including her time spent watching soap operas, when she barely managed to contain her tears during unhappy love scenes.

When the previous month the lady in apartment 104 asked Maria José to sleep in her house, Antonia Maria communicated her distrust to Otávio Pedro, but the latter received the news with evident delight, given that the minor could thereby earn a little more money, and help her parents and younger brothers and sisters, who needed it so much. Moreover, in this way he could sometimes visit Antonia Maria at night, and save the weekly hotel expense on Antonia Maria's free afternoon. Both are trying to save to get married as soon as possible.

Shortly after beginning her job in apartment 104, three weeks approximately, Maria José announced to Antonia Maria that she was pregnant by the watchman. She had achieved her ambition to surrender her virginity to that individual, and now her brother had to intervene in order to make the watchman formalize the relationship, even if only in words, as for example to promise solemnly to live forever with her, a promise that the watchman was to utter in the presence of Antonia Maria and Otávio Pedro, as thought out by the minor, within the extreme limits of her ignorance and inexperience.

Antonia Maria immediately disbelieved Maria José's claim of pregnancy because she knew the date of the latter's periods and certain information the minor gave her did not coincide. That same day the minor broached the subject with her brother, who did not want to listen to Antonia Maria's warnings regarding the truth of the matter. In any case, days later Antonia Maria conjectured that the pregnancy could have already been produced, though not proof of her menstruation, which would not come for some days yet.

Testimony taken today, December 21, 1987, by Sergeant Lucio Freitas Coelho, with the consent of Lieutenant Arnoldo Campos Galvão, who countersign below with the deponents.

12

BUENOS AIRES, JANUARY 5, 1988

My dear friend Silvia:

I'm taking advantage of my nephew Ñato's trip to Rio to send you news of me. There's so much to talk about! But first I want to thank you for all your warm words, there on the sidewalk of your house, before I left in the taxi for the airport. It did me a lot of good, and I'm never going to take those words lightly. Whenever one has a chance to do something good for someone, you should do it, right? And those people needed so much, but the devil had to stick his long nose in.

Speaking of poverty, it's incredible how this Buenos Aires is, beggars all over the place! And with such harsh winters here. At least there the climate helps. That poor girl who had to stay up north is not going to be cold, at least that.

Anyway, Silvia, that's over with, and was nothing compared to the misfortune that awaited me. As soon as I arrived my son told me that Ñato had called that morning from Switzerland saying that my little sister wasn't getting better and even gave signs of getting worse. Ñato had made a date to call the next day at noon, and punctually at twelve the phone rang in my son's study; I was at home.

I had always thought it was a passing affliction; I never wanted to give it any importance, but with that other call I did begin to get alarmed, because Luci had gotten much worse. And that very afternoon, before my son left his office, they called from Lucerne again with the sad news.

Poor Luci, it's as if she had waited for me to return to Buenos Aires, to be surrounded by my loved ones, before she left this world. Can you imagine if I had received the news in Rio, alone as I was?

I asked my son to call you or send you a telegram. In all that confusion, with so many phone calls from other people, I don't remember anymore what they decided to do; I hope my message arrived. A sad message, but it had to be sent.

Ñato will soon tell you in person all the details of our poor little Luci's illness, so I don't need to go into that. About my life here there's not much to say; everything is as it was before. Or rather, it isn't, nothing is as before. Because with the passing away of my Emilsen my life changed; I don't know if I explained to you that her apartment is next door to mine. That's why I saw her all the time, several times a day.

I see her husband, Ignacio, very little because he works far away and leaves very early in the morning, and I do see the kids but only when they're about to rush off to school, or just back, always dying of hunger; they go straight for that refrigerator all the time, I don't know how it manages to stay full. The poor kids are in the hands of a maid, who only comes in the morning; their finances aren't going very well and they barely have enough for that. I think I'll help them out with a monthly allowance, even though Ignacio doesn't like the idea. I'll promise him that I won't butt in.

Besides, there's news: Ignacio is going to marry again. There's a woman he's already been seeing for a while; they hadn't wanted to tell me. But the good thing is that she's already a grown woman, older than Emilsen, his age, fifty-one, and she's never been married.

The truth is, that house needs someone to give it a good cleaning; if Emilsen saw what a mess the servant leaves, she'd turn over in her grave. And the kids are at a difficult age. My fear was that he'd fall in with some young thing who wouldn't even know how to scrub a pot clean. This one looks like she'll be a competent housekeeper.

What impressed me was to find the youngest of Emilsen's kids with a different face already, the beginnings of growing up. Such a perfect little face it was, and now it's all swollen, the nose is like a red pepper. I'm convinced that later on he'll grow into his features, he was my handsomest grandson but he got worse than any of them at that age, that awkward stage, I mean.

The day before yesterday I had a touch of high blood pressure, a good scare, and the first thing I thought of was this kid, whose name is Gilberto. If there's anything I'd like to live to see, it's how he ends up as a little man, with his own face. Because as he is now he's not the adorable baby I remember, nor does he yet have the face he'll wear through life. I'm going to watch what I eat, and try not to get nervous for any old reason, so that I can last another year or so.

Write to me soon and with news of your son. I wish the best for you, affectionately,

Nidia

P.S.: I forgot to answer you about one thing. On the sidewalk when I was leaving for the airport, you asked me what Luci's husband had been like, because always talking about Ferreira you'd never asked her about him. At that moment I had to run, so I'm telling you now. She never mentioned him, because he had been a very intelligent man, older than her, and about thirty-five years ago, no, thirty I think, she was sixty, or if not, she was fifty-something. Well, he had an accident and lost all his mental faculties. Poor Alberto came back as a thing, not a person. Luci spent years and years taking care of someone who wasn't her husband anymore. She was always stuck in the house with him, but she read a lot and watched TV. That saved her. And later we took some little trips together. That's how her life was, with its good moments and its bad moments. More or less like everybody's, nobody gets away with everything. A pity that Luci often had the sensation that it was another woman, not her, who had lived the good moments.

That's terrible, but even worse is to forget completely the good parts and remember only the bad. To get away from that you'd have to go running out to the fields immediately, as poor Wilma does, but if you're stuck in an apartment and it's raining outside, you must quickly start doing something useful, if you can. Put yourself to some use. Sewing, mending, whatever you have at hand. That's the only salvation.

RIO DE JANEIRO, JANUARY 31, 1987

Dearest Nidia:

Forgive me for having taken so long to answer you, but I wanted to talk first to the lady in 205, in Luci's building, in case she had some news of that crazy Ronaldo, or the poor nanny.

I finally ran into her on the street and she has no news of anything. The girl, the nanny I mean, sent a note to her parents saying she's well, working in São Paulo, and that the boy is going to marry her, because the baby is going to be born. But since the poor thing doesn't know how to read or write that doesn't mean much—who knows what the truth is?

Many thanks for remembering my son. He never writes, but once in a while he picks up the phone; I don't know how he pays for it because he talks for hours. Luckily, things are going well for him, he says. I'm already resigned; he likes it there and wants to stay, it's his life. He tells me there's a terrible economic crisis. Here the same thing, and in Argentina another just as bad. Where's all this going to end?

An impulse came over me and I almost flew off to Mexico for Christmas; the ticket would have cost me an arm and a leg, because there were seats only in business class. I almost went but Ferreira called and made it understood that I was abandoning him at the worst moment. So I reacted: I'll go to Mexico, but during my vacation, when I can take advantage and stay almost a month, not five miserable days.

Aside from that, my life's always the same. Ferreira shows up from time to time and tells me his things. Ah, but I just realized you left before Christmas! So I have some big news. The first days of this month he moved to his new "home."

He called me the day before, asking for advice. It was more

than anything an economic matter. It turns out his daughter had asked to bring home her boyfriend, a student from the State of Paraná, who has very little money because he lost his job. Anyway, all as a result of the crisis, they're beginning to close factories and offices here, as in Argentina some years ago. And Ferreira preferred to have the boy stay at their house so that they wouldn't be hanging around sleazy hotels, at any hour of the day or night. That's how today's homes are, Nidia, different from those in your day, right?

But, of course, there was no room in the house for one more. And that's why Ferreira moved to this woman's apartment, far away, but at least he'll have a little peace and quiet. And after the proper time passes he'll get married, not now because it's too soon since the death of his wife.

I must admit that the news affected me quite a bit. For a few days everything looked black to me. But last week he phoned me and came by, just like before, and gave the impression that nothing had happened. The new "wife" teaches in a high school, but at night, not like the one who died, and she gets home always after eleven; the classes go from seven to eleven. Today I'm waiting for him again, while I write you this letter. If he takes his time I'll be able to finish it.

And you know, Nidia, with my busy life I have to make time for so many things. Every night besides I write to my boy. Even if it's only a few lines. It's my new discipline and it's producing results. That way I intend to stay in touch with him. It doesn't matter that he doesn't write back, because when he phones he remembers everything from my letters and that way I feel I don't completely lose him. The contact isn't lost, you see? It's a good system, I don't know why it hadn't occurred to me before. He especially likes me to tell him about my patients, about how the cases are evolving. I've always told him about that and it's always interested him.

I'm going to write him something after Ferreira leaves, I want to tell him about the turn of events with a certain patient today. For me this has already become like a drug; if I don't write that little page to my son I can't sleep. He always tells me the same thing: "Mama, don't take it badly if I don't write to you, because often during the day I chat with you in my imagination, and I comment on all the gossip in your letters."

Well, dear Nidia, lots of hugs, and please write me from time to time,

Silvia

· Hello . . .

· Señora Nidia, please.

· This is me, who's this?

· It's Silvia, how are you?

· Silvia! What a nice surprise! Are you here in Buenos Aires?

· No, I'm calling you from Rio.

· Oh, what an honor . . . Tell me, are you all right?

· Yes, working a lot, that's all. And how's your blood pressure doing?

· Fair. But now the good weather is coming, milder, and that helps. It's been terribly hot this summer. But, of course, then comes winter and that's the worst for me.

· Did you receive my letter?

· Yes, the mail is slow but it arrived. I was just about to answer you.

· Nidia, I really felt like talking to you in any case, to find out how you were doing, but today I have something to tell you . . .

· About Ferreira?

· No, there's nothing new about him, always the same . . .

· What is it, then? Something bad?

· No, that girl Wilma, Ronaldo's wife, showed up here in Leblon.

· Oh . . .

· She's already working in a house, the same one where she worked before, over two years ago, I think. But they like her a lot there, and when she arrived they immediately took her on.

· Oh, I see . . .

· She came to see if she could find her husband; she's pretty desperate about that. She came to my house to ask me questions.

· Poor girl . . .

· She asked a lot after you, Nidia . . .

· I see . . .

· She badly needs support, she looked bad, really desperate.

· Poor thing . . .

· Nidia, why don't you come when it starts getting cold in Buenos Aires? Luci's apartment still hasn't been rented.

· And why doesn't anybody take it? It's so nice!

· It's just that your nephew left orders with the real estate office that aren't realistic, Nidia; he's asking for a lot, he's thinking in terms of Switzerland.

· But I'm not up to any more such carrying on, Silvia.

· Your family won't say anything, now that it's starting to get cold in Buenos Aires.

· No, Silvia, really, I don't have any energy for that.

· It's that I started to worry about the girl, this Wilma.

· Give her a hug from me, please.

· Now, you know, Nidia, we'd always welcome you with open arms here.

· Thanks, really, but I don't think it can be done. I've got a lot of years on me.

· Call me whenever you want, I'm here, I'm not going to Mexico till vacation time in July.

· No, Silvia. I made a mistake once and I'm not going to repeat it. I can't trust that kind of people.

· Yes, I understand, but . . .

· No, I'm not going back there again.

· Think it over, and if not . . . someday I'll show up in Buenos Aires.

· You would? That would be wonderful, come soon!

· No, Nidia, I just meant that . . . There's not enough time; it's already too much with my trip to Mexico, and I have to take care of my patients.

· I don't know, Silvia, you sound sort of sad.

· It's homesickness, Nidia, everybody who matters to me is so far away.

· Do you see Ferreira often?

· Usually once a week, the day his wife finishes up later at school.

· What day of the week, if I'm not being too nosy?

· Wednesdays. It's a good day, isn't it? Because it divides the week in two.

· Last night, then. But he didn't come, right?

· Right.

· Ah . . .

· You always guess everything. Well, it's once every two weeks, really. And if Wednesday happens to fall on a holiday . . . it's even worse. He's stuck with her at home.

· That's very little, every once in a while.

· I think so. Well, nice to know you're well, lots of hugs.

· And is the weather nice?

· Yes, though night falls around five, the days are getting shorter.

· Silvia . . . forgive my butting in, but . . . why don't you tell that Ferreira to go to hell?

· I was about to. There was one thing that caught my attention. Every time I mentioned the Mexico trip to him he became grouchy.

· Men can be so self-centered.

· But I liked that, he seemed to be rejecting my trip because he would miss me.

· That's true, in his own way he loves you, I've always thought. He's a good person, you don't have to rack your brains trying to figure him out. But with him it's here today, gone tomorrow, so if you're not comfortable with that . . . send him packing for good!

· There was something about packing that came up, you know, Nidia? But it's all nonsense, I'd just bore you.

· No, it's not nonsense, now I want to know, Silvia, tell me, please!

· It's just that since he didn't want us to be separated, for me to go away on vacation, I began to get my hopes up again, that he might love me . . . more than it appears, more than he shows. But on the other hand, since any silly thing would keep him from coming over, that contradiction bothered me. So I set a trap for the poor thing . . .

· I'm listening.

· I told him one day that perhaps I wouldn't be going to Mexico after all, for lack of time. I was lying, of course. And that I hadn't paid for that ticket, that it was a government invitation, and that I could very easily transfer it to his name, that he should take advantage of it, and . . . start packing.

· Oh no, Silvia, don't tell me . . .

· Yes, I'm telling you. I was waiting for him to say, "Great! Don't go, stay with me in Rio!" But it didn't work out that way, he jumped with joy, and not because I was staying but because he'd be able to travel!

· How disgusting . . .

· It made him angry that I could go. He was jealous, but not of me, of the trip!

· Oh, Silvia, I don't think he deserves you, then. I thought he was better than that, more magnanimous.

· He's good, Nidia. But he has that problem inside, that frustration, over not having lived. It makes him angry that others can do things.

· You understand him, which is maybe why he takes advantage of you.

· I do do that a bit, perhaps it's professional deformity that causes me to make excuses for people too much.

· Yes, but he takes advantage and gives you nothing in return.

· Well, I wouldn't go that far. He does communicate things to me that are very positive. It must be that desire of his to live, that accumulated, retroactive desire. So few people have such an illusion about things. He's convinced that by taking that trip, everything would be marvelous, those trips he dreams of . . . It's infectious, he makes me feel like joining him on that ship that departs from who knows where, I mean fishing boat or whatever he calls it, I don't know its exact name. He always says it in his Brazilian slang. Oh well, I'm forgetting my native language.

· And me the little bit of Portuguese I learned.

· It's not a big boat, it's some other word . . .

· It may be a raft.

· No, a raft is too simple a thing. But it doesn't matter!

Even if it were only a raft, I'd hop on with him. A raft going nowhere. Or somewhere, maybe.

· I don't know what to say to you, Silvia, it's not easy to give you advice. To get into that . . . rowboat, or not.

· You won't believe it but you are helping me already, just talking to you is helpful. It's good to talk, it clears things up in my mind. But one can't talk to just anyone.

· As long as you won't regret it when the phone bill arrives.

· No, Nidia, if only all my problems were about money. No, the Ferreira thing is so important to me, talking to you now I have a better idea about what's going on, which is that when I'm with him . . . his enthusiasm is infectious, and I feel convinced that the raft does go somewhere, to a safe port. But when I'm alone I begin to doubt, and it's terrible to think that nothing goes anywhere.

·   . . .

· You're not talking, Nidia.

· I know, I'd like so much to say something right, to help you, but nothing comes to mind.

·   . . .

· Now you're the one who's not talking.

· I know . . .

· But one thing does come to mind! Don't you go paying for a trip to Mexico for that good-for-nothing!

· No, no way! Besides, there he'd be in my way. There I want the company of my son.

· He'd really be in your way there?

· Of course. A month will be barely enough time to take decent care of my son, poor kid. You know how we mothers are. And to see all my friends from years back. There's still a few Argentine exiles hanging around there.

· Ah . . .

· Does that seem wrong to you?

· I don't know if I got it straight. You wouldn't like to travel to Mexico with Ferreira?

· No! What do I want him there for? Here's where I need a little affection!

·   . . .

· You're not talking again, Nidia.

· No, I was just thinking, that's all.

· The bell rang, the patient's here already.

· Well, Silvia, write to me always.

· And your grandson, did his nose shrink?

· I don't know, Silvia, I haven't seen him for days.

· Well, Nidia, a kiss, and I hope I'll see you soon.

· A big hug, and thanks for remembering me.

· And if I see Wilma, shall I give her a message from you?

· Yes, that I'm very sorry about what happened.

· Ciao, see you . . . And come, Nidia, you'll be very well received.

· No, Silvia, no travel for me, that's completely out of the question.

· What a pity. A hug . . .

· Ciao, Silvia.

AEROLÍNEAS ARGENTINAS
Flight Report / Passenger Service

DATE: February 24, 1988
FLIGHT: 401 Buenos Aires–New York with one stop in Rio de Janeiro
STEWARD ON BOARD: Raúl Costanzo

The only irregularity recorded during the flight took place before landing in Rio de Janeiro, where the passenger from tourist class N. de Angelis, already assigned special attention because of her advanced age and high blood pressure, was disembarking. Her salt-free dinner had been served to her accordingly, and the passenger expressed satisfaction with the treatment received. Shortly before landing in Rio, stewardess Ana María Ziehl approached me with a dilemma: she had noticed the above-mentioned passenger hiding in her ample handbag one of our flight blankets. Stewardess Ziehl had not dared to point out to the passenger that the blanket was the property of Aerolíneas Argentinas, given the passenger's age and condition, but she did mention it to the writer of this report. By common agreement it was decided to ignore the incident. In any case, evidence of the episode is recorded to illustrate the problem of the constant disappearance of blankets. The landing in Rio was particularly smooth, and the passengers applauded the captain's skill.